ATTACK NEW YORK!

by

Duncan Harding

THUNDERCHILD PUBLISHING
Huntsville, Alabama

This book is a work of fiction. Any references to historical events, real people, or real places are used fictitiously. Other names, characters, places, and events are products of the author's imagination, and any resemblance to actual events or places or persons, living or dead, is entirely coincidental.

ATTACK NEW YORK!

Copyright © 1994 by Duncan Harding.

Published by arrangement with the Charles Whiting literary estate.

All rights reserved. No part of this publication may be reproduced, stored in a retrieval system, or transmitted in any form or by any means, electronic, mechanical, photocopying, recording or otherwise, without the written permission of the publisher.

ISBN: 9781092112468

Published by Thunderchild Publishing. Find us at https://ourworlds.net/thunderchild_cms/

AUTHOR'S NOTE

I would like to thank fellow author Charles Whiting for his assistance on the factual side of this novel. His books *The March in London* (Leo Cooper Ltd 1992) and *Skorzeny* (Pan-Ballantine 1992) have proved especially valuable.

DH

EPIGRAPH

So far the American people — of all peoples of this war — have never felt the war in their homeland ... It is my earnest wish that they shall get a taste of the war before very long.

Adolf Hitler, October 1944

Extract from the *Boston Globe* June 16, 1993.

GERMANY WANTS TO LET A SLEEPING SUB LIE:
PREFERS U-BOAT BE LEFT IN CAPE WATERS

by James Arnold, *Globe* staff.

Edward Michaud, the diver who claims with a Rhode Island technician to have found the wreck of a German U-boat in shallow water off Cape Cod, said yesterday he hoped one day to raise the U-1226. But a spokesman for the German government said he preferred to leave the submarine and the remains of the sailors at rest.

Speaking about the find in public for the first time, Michaud said the U-1226 was in a squadron of four submarines linked to "quite an active spy ring" of Nazis operating from Cape Cod during the Second World War. Michaud said he knew there would be many obstacles to raising the boat.

For example, according to Friedo Sielemann, press attaché to the German Consulate in Boston, the German government considers the submarine German property and a war grave best left alone. "But in this case such a policy may be impractical because the boat appears to be so accessible," Sielemann added.

The submarine lies in just forty-one feet of water about four miles east of Cape Cod according to Paul Matthias, the president of Polaris Consulting Inc of Narragansett, RI. His highly sophisticated sonar imaging instruments helped Michaud locate the 250-foot sub on June 5.

He and Michaud said they were being intentionally vague about the wreck's location to protect it from "the few bad apples" in the marine salvage business.

Michaud, a commercial diver from Framingham, described the moment of discovery as Matthias' equipment outlined the submarine as bitter-sweet. "There was no jumping up and down on deck. Mixed with enthusiasm was our awareness for the tremendous loss of life aboard," Michaud said during a press briefing aboard the vessel *Odyssey* in Boston Harbor. "The submarine was carrying more than fifty sailors and spies when it got caught transmitting on a US Coast Guard frequency on October 29, 1944," according to Michaud. Within minutes aircraft from the Hyannis Naval Squadron bombed and sank the submarine.

Michaud added he had "absolutely precise confirmation" from Germany and American sources that the submarine is the U-1226 and that it was on spy duty. Some of the information from the Navy about the submarine remains classified according to Michaud. He did not know if the submarine had just picked up spies or was about to drop them off when it was bombed.

Michaud was questioned about the whereabouts of the other three German U-boats, but he could provide no answer to that query. He was also asked at the press conference what were the Germans attempting to spy on in the USA in late 1944 when GIs were already across the Reich's frontiers and it was obvious that that country had lost the war. Again, Navy veteran Michaud could not provide an answer.

So as sunbathers along the beaches here flip through John Grisham's latest thriller, Cape Cod has been caught up in a real summer mystery: *What happened to those other Jerry subs and what had they crossed 3,000 miles of the Atlantic to do?*

CHATHAM, MASS.

ONE

SKORZENY

ONE

Above the men waiting in the pre-dawn cold, silently puffing at their last cigarettes, the stark outline of the Hungarian castle which housed the traitor was silhouetted against the dirty white autumn sky. In front of them was the steep winding Wienerstrasse. They would take it soon. Now it lay silent and empty. But the waiting men in the black uniforms of the German Panzertruppe and the camouflage smocks of the SS knew that meant nothing. The Wienerstrasse was barricaded and mined. Picked Hungarian troops, their supposed Allies, were waiting in the dark houses on both sides to walk straight into the trap.

Up front the SS giant with the terrible scarred face rose up in the Volkswagen jeep. He towered above his bodyguard of NCOs hung with stick grenades and extra magazines for their automatics. He frowned. At this moment his force seemed very small for the task he had soon to undertake: four tanks, a troop of Goliaths — mini remote-controlled tracked vehicles each packed with 500 pounds of high explosive — and two companies of SS parachute infantry. But he knew the job had to be done. Although the fortress above was reputedly held by a whole Hungarian division he had to capture the traitor who was about to betray the Fuhrer and take Hungary out of the war on Germany's side. Success was vital. If Hungary fell the Russians would push even further westwards.

The SS giant looked at his most prized possession. It was a watch given to him as a reward by the Italian dictator Mussolini the year before. Then he had rescued the dictator from the mountain prison where he had been held and returned him to Germany. That had won him the Knight's Cross of the Iron Cross and the command of the SS's most élite unit, *das Jagdkommando* *. "It's Mussolini time," he cried, using the old joke he always used when he referred to the gift watch, "Zero six hundred hours. *Los!*"

His élite reacted at once. Hurriedly the infantry sprang aboard the vehicles. The dawn stillness was shattered by motors bursting into life. Drivers gunned their cold engines. There could be no stalling on that winding road ahead. The air was suddenly full of the stink of diesel. Men clicked off their safety catches. The tank gunners swung their long cannon round like the snouts of predatory monsters seeking their prey.

SS Obersturmbannfuhrer Otto Skorzeny touched his Knight's Cross one last time for luck and then cried, *"Vorwaerts, Leute!"*

His driver thrust home first gear. The Volkswagen Jeep lurched forward. Behind it the rest of the tense apprehensive column followed. Operation Bazooka had commenced ...

He had come to the Hungarian capital, Budapest, the week before. Disguised as a Dr Wolf he had been sent to the capital by Hitler. His brief was to find out whether Admiral Horthy, the Hungarian dictator, was secretly preparing to make a separate peace with their common enemy, Russia.

It had not taken "Dr Wolf" long to find out that Horthy was talking with the Russians. He decided to act immediately. He would capture Horthy's darling playboy son Miki. He would be used as a hostage to keep Hungary in the war. It was the kind of spirited bold stroke, using a handful of picked men, which had always appealed to Skorzeny.

Thus, on a peaceful autumn Sunday afternoon, Dr Wolf and a few "friends" drove up to the quiet square where Miki Horthy had his residence. The place was almost empty save for Hungarian trucks parked outside the house. A little further on there was a canvas-backed Hungarian army truck and Miki's private Mercedes.

Dr Wolf had parked and had pretended to fiddle beneath the hood of his own car. Across the way the canvas hood of the truck was jerked back. Someone was checking what the scarfaced giant

---

* Equivalent to the SAS.

was up to. Skorzeny risked a quick look. He caught a glimpse of a heavy machinegun mounted on a tripod. The traitors, he told himself, were prepared for trouble.

A couple of German military police, carbines slung over their shoulders, strolled into the square. It looked as if they were just on a boring routine patrol. Suddenly, startlingly, they lost their air of bored unconcern. They tugged down their weapons and began to run for the house. The Hungarians reacted. They flung back the canvas. A machinegun spat fire. One of the MPs yelped with pain and went down heavily on the cobbles. He had been hit in the leg. Skorzeny cursed and rushing out into the line of fire, grabbed the wounded cop by the scruff of the neck and dragged him to safety.

Shouting wildly, Hungarian troops started to flood into the square. Skorzeny, abandoning his pose now, shrilled a swift blast on his whistle. His paras rushed from their hiding places, firing their pistols as they ran. Skorzeny's driver cursed and slammed to the cobbles. The Hungarian machinegun was proving too much for the attackers. Soon, Skorzeny knew, his handful would be overrun. He had to call up his main body.

He blew two shrill blasts on his whistle. Under the command of his adjutant the rest of his troop sprang into action. The sight of the Germans pelting towards them took the heart out of the Hungarians. They started to back off.

An excited, red-faced Skorzeny didn't give them a chance to recover. *"Los!"* he yelled above the angry snap-and-crack of the small arms fight. "After me — the captain's got a hole in his arse!" He darted forward, firing his pistol, snapping off shots to left and right. Behind him his paras started to lob stick grenades at the Hungarians as up above them Hungarian soldiers on the roof of the house tugged off great chunks of masonry and hurled them down on the attackers.

But the unusual weapons didn't stop Skorzeny and his men. Within minutes they had burst through the door and were inside the house, panting and flushed, to find the Germans they had already planted inside the house had already captured young Horthy and were holding him at pistol point.

The Hungarian playboy, crimson with anger, was waving his hands about in rage. "I'll have you all executed," he cried. "Don't you know who my father is ... My God, this is an outrage ... I order you to release me at once."

Desperately Skorzeny looked around for some means of silencing Horthy. He didn't want to use physical violence on this precious hostage. His gaze flashed around the big salon. Then he had it. His gaze fell on the large flowered carpet at his feet. "Put him in that," he yelled, "and tie the damned thing up with that piece of curtain rope. At the double now! *Dalli!*"

The paras, grinning all over their burly faces at the dodge, pushed the wildly gesticulating Hungarian playboy down to the carpet. In an instant his protests were muffled. Like some victim in a child's book he was trundled round and round on the floor as the paras whipped the cord around him. Seconds later the playboy lay trussed like an animal being prepared for the market, twitching and wriggling wildly, but unable to get out of the carpet.

Skorzeny grinned at his adjutant. "All right, to the airport with our dear playboy ... and remember, no more shooting, understood?"

His adjutant grinned back and nodded to his men to pick up the human bundle. Operation Mickey Mouse, as it had been called, had taken exactly ten minutes. Now the question was how would the playboy's father, Admiral Horthy, react?

Back at his hotel HQ Skorzeny chain-smoked nervously, taking an occasional sip at his brandy, waiting for the news. Messengers came and went. Their news was not good. Horthy's residence had been completely sealed off. Heavily armed troops were appearing everywhere in Budapest. Roads were barred and minefields were being laid on all key roads.

Then, as Skorzeny sweated it out knowing that Miki Horthy was now on his way to the Reich, Radio Budapest cut into its normal programmes. The speaker, obviously flustered and excited, blurted out that the Hungarian nation should stand by for an important announcement by Admiral Horthy at two o'clock that afternoon.

Two o'clock came. An anxious Skorzeny, his officers and an interpreter craned their necks forward to catch every word that came from the pear-shaped "People's Radio". The Admiral pulled no punches. He launched an angry tirade against Hitler and his German allies. Germany, he declared firmly, despite the knowledge that he might be condemning his favourite son to death with his words, had lost the war. There was no hope for the Fatherland.

The officers flushed angrily when the interpreters translated the Admiral's statement. Hurriedly Skorzeny held up his hand for silence. "Quiet, *meine Herren,* quiet, please. Let us hear what the old fool has to say."

"Hungary must now leave the war," the Admiral went on, "I have already asked for an armistice from the Russians. Hostilities between the Hungarian Army and the Red Army will cease at once."

"Great crap on the Christmas tree!" Skorzeny snorted angrily, and he flung his glass at the wall where it shattered. He had gambled and failed. The daring kidnap scheme had come to naught. All that was left was Operation Bazooka.

Now, two days later, the little SS convoy ground its way up the hill. Next to Skorzeny, his adjutant whispered tensely, lips suddenly very dry, "Bit unpleasant if we caught a packet from the flank, Obersturmbannfuhrer, eh?"

Skorzeny didn't answer. The giant's heart was thudding. Any moment he expected his Jeep would hit one of the mines that spies had reported laid on the road. But nothing happened.

He wet his lips. "Go faster," he whispered to his driver. He pumped his brawny right arm up and down three times. It was the signal for those behind to do the same.

It was growing lighter. Hungarian sentries started to appear from the shadows. All of them were heavily armed. Skorzeny forced himself to wave to them happily. The Hungarians clicked to attention. Skorzeny swallowed hard. The Hungarians suspected nothing. They were through the first barrier.

Now they were rolling towards Horthy's residence at twenty miles an hour. In the milky light Skorzeny could see three Hungarian tanks parked outside. They were buttoned up, ready for action. Would they fire?

Suddenly the first of the three tanks raised its long-barrelled 75 mm cannon high into the air. That indicated it wouldn't fire. "Heaven, arse and cloudburst!" Skorzeny cursed to his adjutant. "We're doing it. For God's sake we're doing it!"

They rolled on.

They turned another bend in the steep winding cobbled road. A barricade loomed up. This time they were out of luck. The Hungarians manning it raised their weapons. They were going to fire.

Skorzeny signalled to the Panther tank behind him. Its driver accelerated. At top speed the big tank rolled forward. It smashed into the barricade. The barricade disintegrated to reveal six anti-tank guns, all manned, hidden behind it.

Skorzeny didn't wait to see if they would fire on his tanks. He sprang out of the jeep tugging his pistol from the holster as he did so. *"Dalli ... dalli!"* he cried urgently, pelting forward, followed by his adjutant and bodyguard.

Whistles shrilled. Frantic NCOs bellowed orders. A siren started to wail its urgent warning. A bare-headed Hungarian colonel waving a pistol ran at them. The adjutant slammed his fist into the man's face. The pistol flew from his hand. They ran on. Another Hungarian, half dressed, came into view. Skorzeny grabbed him panting madly. "Lead us to the Commandant — *at once!"* he ordered.

The half-dressed Hungarian hesitated. Skorzeny smashed the fist holding the pistol into his face. His nose broke. Hot sticky red blood spurted over the giant's knuckles. "Please don't hit me again," the man stammered thickly. *"Please!"* He turned and started up the steps.

They moved into the fortress, the sound of gunfire muted by the ancient thick walls. No one attempted to bar their way. Skorzeny rushed into a big room. A Hungarian was crouched behind a machine-gun at the window. With a grunt Sergeant Holzer, his bodyguard, pushed by him. "Give me that peashooter," he panted. With one and the same movement he picked up the heavy machinegun and threw it through the window. Tamely the gunner surrendered.

Another room and another, the place was a maze of dark passages and rooms heavy with the ornaments and fading paintings of another age. Another door. Surprisingly enough Skorzeny, his huge chest heaving with the effort of so much running and fighting, knocked on it. Later he could never explain why.

A soldier in the dress of a Hungarian major-general opened it. "Are you the Commandant?" Skorzeny snapped.

The general's mouth dropped open stupidly as he stared up at the giant with his scarred face that looked like the work of a butcher gone mad. He seemed unable to speak.

Skorzeny lost patience with the fool. "I demand you surrender at once," he bellowed in the Hungarian general's face. "You are responsible if any more blood is shed. I ask you for an *immediate* decision!"

Tamely the general let his shoulders sag in defeat. "I surrender to you," he said in his soft Hungarian German. "I will order immediate cessations of hostilities." Thereupon he thrust out his hand.

Surprised, Skorzeny took it. At the cost of twenty casualties he had captured the traitor Admiral Horthy, for whom a special train was already waiting at Budapest station, steam raised, ready to transport him to the Reich where he would be "guest of the Fuhrer" from now on. Hungary would stay in the war at Germany's side. All in all, it had been a tremendous coup.

He beamed at his officers and cried, "I know it's early, gentlemen, but let's get drunk. I think we've deserved it." With his pistol he shot off the neck of a bottle of wine resting on the table next to the ashen-faced Hungarian general. The latter jumped but the scarfaced giant didn't notice. He grabbed the bottle with his paw of a hand and started gulping down the fine Tokay wine greedily.

TWO

"Das haben Sie gut gemacht, lieber Skorzeny," Hitler said as the guards outside the bunker clicked to attention. In the Austrian fashion, for both of them had been born in that country, he took the giant's hand in both of his own and gave it a feeble shake.

Still holding the giant's hand, Hitler led him inside the bunker followed only by his Alsatian bitch, Blondi. He offered Skorzeny a seat and said, his voice weak still from the bomb attack made on him the previous July, "Tell me about the Hungarian business, my dear Skorzeny."

Sitting rigidly at attention as military protocol prescribed, Skorzeny described the events of the previous week. Once Hitler laughed when the SS man explained how they had bundled Miki Horthy into a carpet to shut him up. *"Grossartig ...* capital!" he exclaimed, a new strength in his voice suddenly. "That's the way to treat those damned traitors!"

Finally Skorzeny finished and again, as protocol prescribed, he rose to his feet to depart, but Hitler shook his head. His face thoughtful and pensive, as if he had something important on his mind, he commanded, "Stay awhile, Skorzeny, I have something to tell you."

The SS man sat down again his mind racing electrically. So he hadn't been invited to the Fuhrer's HQ for a chat and a cup of coffee with some new medal thrown in for good measure. The Fuhrer had a new mission for him. He knew that instinctively. He waited in tense expectation. For a moment or two the Fuhrer remained silent as if considering whether he really should disclose what was going on in his mind at this moment. Inside the bunker there was no sound save that of the dog snoring at Hitler's feet. From outside there came the crisp crunching of the sentries' boots on the gravel paths as they patrolled the area around the Fuhrer's bunker.

Finally Hitler broke the heavy brooding silence. "Skorzeny," he said, his voice excited, "I am going to give you the most important mission of your life." Skorzeny felt his heart begin to race. He waited. "So far only very few people know of my preparations ... the secret plan in which you will play a great role." He paused to let his words sink in. Hitler's eyes sparkled and a little colour flushed his pale sunken cheeks. "Skorzeny," he announced, "in December Germany will commence a great offensive which will be decisive for the future of our country."

Skorzeny suppressed a gasp but his face must have revealed his shock at the news. Germany was on her knees. The Russians were only a few kilometres from the very bunker in which they now sat. The Anglo-Americans were already fighting on Germany's soil. Why, the old German Imperial city of Aachen had just fallen to the Americans. Yet the Fuhrer was talking about going on the offensive again!

"I know, I know, *mein lieber,*" Hitler said, seeing that look of shocked surprise on the other man's scarred face. "The world thinks Germany is finished with only the day and the hour of the funeral to be arranged. But I am going to show just how mistaken they are. The corpse will rise and hurl itself in fury at the West. Then we shall see."

The West, Skorzeny registered the words quickly. So Hitler was going to attack the Anglo-American plutocrats and not the Red Army. So far most of his work had been against the Russians. He knew little of the Tommies and their allies, the Amis.

For an hour Hitler poured out the details of his great plan while Skorzeny listened, awestruck. He discovered that Hitler had raised a great new army a million strong by combing out the Navy and the Air Force, turfing out students from their universities and the lightly wounded from the hospitals. Whole headquarters had been closed down and the men sent to this new army which was being armed with the latest weapons pouring from Germany's secret underground factories. It had apparently been a *levée en masse* which had cleared the Reich of virtually every male between the ages of sixteen and forty-five.

Skorzeny listened amazed, greedily drinking in the details of the new divisions, fighter squadrons, tank brigades, fresh hope springing up at the knowledge that Germany wasn't finished; they still had a chance to beat the greatest coalition the world had ever seen.

Finally Hitler said, "I have told you so much so that you will realise that everything has been considered very carefully. *Everything* has been worked out to the last detail."

Skorzeny nodded his understanding and wondered if the Fuhrer would now tell him what his part in this great new offensive in the West would be. The Fuhrer obliged.

"You are to be given a very important role, for which you will receive a document signed by my own hand empowering you to take any measure you think fit — in the Fuhrer's name. Now, only a few days ago I received word that Americans wearing German uniforms were involved in action against Aachen. Well, Skorzeny, two can play that kind of game. You will raise a whole brigade which will drive captured American vehicles, wear captured American uniforms and speak English. These troops will be based behind the American lines in France, Belgium and Luxemburg. They will capture key roads and bridges, destroy enemy communications, give false orders etc etc."

Skorzeny's mind raced. The Fuhrer was ordering him to activate a brigade of spies and saboteurs, men who would risk being shot if captured in enemy uniform. "Aber mein Fuhrer" he prepared to protest against the order. But as always when he was set on an idea, Hitler never listened.

"But there is more, Skorzeny," he went on swiftly while at his feet Blondi continued to snore. "I want you to take the war to the enemy homeland. For years those air gangsters, the Anglo-Americans, have destroyed our cities, killing our civilians by the hundred thousand, poor innocent old men, women and children. Now the time has come for them to pay — *on* their own doorstep." He rose to his feet and Blondi grunted in protest. "Let me show you this map." He crossed to a curtain covering one of the many maps on the walls of the bunker. With a flourish he drew the curtain aside.

"England," he announced as Skorzeny stared at the map of the United Kingdom dotted with a rash of red pins.

"Each one of those pins represents one of their POW camps holding German prisoners. In all there are a quarter of a million of them, fit determined young men, all from the fighting arms of the Wehrmacht — paratroopers, infantry, tankers and the like. Now, my dear fellow, right in the heart of the enemy camp we have the equivalent of a whole army." He beamed at the giant, "Surely we can use that army, made up of men whose most fervent desire is to be free and return to their beloved homeland?"

"But they are prisoners, *mein* Fuhrer," Skorzeny protested, utterly confused by this time.

"In effect, yes, *at the present*. But they are guarded by old men and those who have been severely wounded, invalids in other words, just the same type as those who guard our prisoners here. They would be no match against our splendid fellows once they were armed."

Skorzeny opened his mouth to say something, then thought better of it.

Hitler smiled. "You are, of course, wondering where all this is leading, aren't you?"

"Yes, *mein* Fuhrer."

"Well, intelligence has reported we are in touch with those POWs in every camp throughout the country. It has been done by code, secret wireless transmitters and special soldiers who were briefed what to do before they were captured. The English allow their prisoners a great deal of freedom. They think a German would be unable to escape. After all, that damned country *is* an island. So they work on the land in factories and learn where the enemy keeps his arms dumps, his tank parks and the like." Hitler's eyes twinkled. "You see what I mean, Skorzeny?"

"I do, I do, *mein* Fuhrer," Skorzeny blurted out. "It's a kind ... a kind of Trojan Horse."

"Exactly."

"But what could we do with those men, *mein* Fuhrer?"

"Not *we,* but *you*. It is going to be another of your tasks, to ensure that when the great offensive commences there is an uprising in every camp in England, timed to coincide with the attack. Imagine what panic and confusion that will start in the enemy's camp. Thousands of armed German soldiers on the rampage throughout England. The whole of the Tommy's infrastructure will break down. What reinforcements the Anglo-Americans still have stationed on that island will be unable to reach the continent. They will have to be employed in quelling the uprising in their midst. You see the beauty of the scheme?"

"*Jawohl, mein* Fuhrer," Skorzeny snapped, telling himself that Adolf Hitler had not lost his capacity for pulling a surprise rabbit out of the top hat. "It is, with permission, a splendid idea."

"I am glad you like it," Hitler said, obviously pleased with Skorzeny's reaction. "It has been a long war and we Germans have suffered some grievous blows over these last five years. But if we can retain our faith in our holy cause and use the brains that the good God has seen to bestow on our Germans, we can still triumph, achieve that final victory that the German people so heartily deserves."

Skorzeny rose quickly to his feet, body erect, hand extended in salute. *"Sieg Heil!"* he bellowed enthusiastically at the top of his voice as if he were back on the parade ground.

"Heil," Hitler said casually, flapping up a weak, limp hand. "But not so hasty, my dear fellow. There is one other project which I wish you to take charge of."

"One more?"

"Yes, one which is the dearest to my heart, I think. Come, there is another map I wish you to look at." He crossed to the opposite wall and Blondi, who had settled down once more into her doggy dream world, growled a little impatiently and opened one baleful eye.

Again Hitler drew aside the little curtain covering the new map which was also marked *"Reichsgeheimsache",* Imperial Top Secret.

Skorzeny peered at the map, which showed some kind of seaboard. But he could not recognise anything, although he had travelled ever much of Europe in these last few years, for there were no names printed on this strange map. Bunched tightly together in an area of perhaps some fifty square kilometres were clustered together the same sort of red pins he had spotted on the other map

Hitler smiled patiently at Skorzeny's obvious bewilderment. "You don't recognise the area, I presume," he said indulgently.

"No, I confess I don't, *mein* Fuhrer," Skorzeny admitted, still searching the terrain for any kind of a clue.

"Well, I shall enlighten you, Obersturmbannfuhrer."

"Sir?"

"It is the coast of the United States of America, the east coast to be exact, not far from the birthplace of that Jewish plutocrat who currently rules that Continent."

"You mean Roosevelt, *mein* Fuhrer."

"Yes, the Jew Roosevelt, who was born — curse the day — here," Hitler stabbed the map not far from where the red pins clustered in profusion.

Skorzeny's bewilderment increased. Why was the map unmarked? What did the red pins signify this time? Why was the Fuhrer taking so much interest in the place where the American President, Roosevelt, had been born in the last century? Above all, what had all this got to do with him?

"You are puzzled, dear Skorzeny," Hitler said, "I can see that. And so you should be. I hope, too, the enemy will remain as puzzled as you are at this moment until it is too late. You see, we are going to do something which the Japanese failed to do in '42 and '43."

"I see," Skorzeny said, though he didn't see at all.

"Then, Japanese planes launched from submarines off the American west coast attempted to launch firebombs at some of the huge forests of that coast. The attack wasn't a success. A year later they floated balloons on the prevailing winds all the way across the Pacific to the west coast. They were timed to go off at certain junctures. Again the aim was to set fire to the American forests. Only two succeeded and little damage was done. Thereafter, our allies gave up trying to take the war to America." He let the information sink in before saying, "But the idea was excellent. So far the Americans — of all peoples of this war — have never felt the war in their homeland and being the racial mishmash they are — Jews, Niggers, Italians and the like — they will panic once they taste what war is like." He smiled at Skorzeny, "It is my earnest wish that they get a taste of the war before very long. I —" He stopped short

20

abruptly. On the floor Blondi pricked up her ears and began to whine softly. From the east there came the first shrill wail of the air-raid sirens. Hurriedly Hitler walked to his desk and picked up his cap as Blondi cowered at his feet. Now Skorzeny could hear the sharp crack and boom of the flak guns.

"Come," Hitler commanded as his guards opened the door from outside, one of them already bearing a steel helmet for the Fuhrer. "The Reds are about to pay us a visit. The rest and most interesting part of your mission must wait till later." Then, seizing the helmet and putting it on over his cap, he hobbled as fast as he could for the air-raid shelter with Blondi, her tail tucked between her legs, running with him.

THREE

"Here they come, the shitehawks ... Off the port bow!" the angry hoarse voice cried against the howling wind. "Shitting Sunderlands!"

Everywhere the weary bearded submariners tumbled from their bunks or rushed to their duty stations as the U-boat's klaxon howled its dire warning.

The big lumbering British flying boats were coming in their usual formation, some flying high to attract the U-boat's flak while the rest came in skimming across the grey North Sea, churning the water to a white fury with their prop wash. It would be their job to attempt to torpedo the enemy shipping.

Down in his cramped little cabin Kapitanleutnant Brandt cursed heartily as the dread wail of emergency siren filled the stinking hull of his boat. He had hoped to enter the Kattegat and sail into the Baltic without being spotted. But these days the Tommies dominated the sky. And there was no use attempting to dive. The sea was too shallow just here where the North Sea met the Baltic. Hastily he screwed on his damned wooden arm, which he hated passionately, tugged on his white cap and thrust his way through the crowded U-boat, which stank of unwashed bodies, stale food and diesel oil. He clattered up the ladder into the conning tower already aware that the twin MGs were hammering away, sending a thousand slugs a minute skywards.

"They're coming fast, the bastards," Degenhardt his first officer snapped, noticing, as usual, there was no sign of fear in the skipper's thin, pale hawk-like face. But then Kapitanleutnant Brandt was an old hare — a veteran who had survived this sort of thing a dozen times.

Brandt flung his glasses with his good hand. "Brandt's Wolf Pack", as his U-boat flotilla was known throughout the German Navy, was keeping the correct formation. It was spread over four square kilometres, the gunners firing to each side, bringing their aim closer as the Tommies came on in. Then he swept the sky with his binoculars. The lookout had been right: the ten flying boats were evenly divided, five at some height the others at sea level.

Suddenly he cursed, "By the great whore of Buxtehude where the dogs piss through the ribs!" he roared.

"What is it, sir?" Degenhardt yelled above the frenetic hysterical chatter of the machineguns.

"Starboard!" Brandt snapped laconically as the gleaming silver metal shapes slid effortlessly into the calibrated circles of his glasses.

"Verdammte Scheisse!" the first officer cursed as he recognised the fat-bellied American planes with their big radial engines. "Thunderbolts!"

"Right in one. They were trying to take us by sur —" The rest of Brandt's words were drowned by the roar of a bomb exploding. Abruptly the U-boat heeled and reeled as the water boiled to left and right of the small craft. Brandt gasped and closed his eyes momentarily as the blast struck him in the face like a blow from a flabby, damp hand. Down at the deck gun one of the gunners screamed in agony and went over the side, arms flailing wildly. When he hit the water it coloured red immediately with his blood.

Now, as the bombs exploded all around the little U-boat flotilla and the guns blasted away, peppering the grey dawn sky with puffs of angry black smoke, the Thunderbolts hovered over the submarines momentarily. To Brandt they looked like sinister metal hawks. Then, with frightening suddenness, the flight leader flung himself out of the sky.

With its engine howling madly the fighter-bomber hurtled straight downwards as if intent on plunging into the sea. Flak exploded all around it. Twice Brandt thought the American plane had been hit; twice he was mistaken. The tough American plane still came hurtling down, ready for the kill.

Suddenly the Thunderbolt staggered visibly. Bright lights crackled the length of its wings. "For what we are about to receive," Degenhardt chanted, "Let the Lord make us truly thankful."

Whoosh! In a white fury great fiery rockets slashed through the grey dawn. To port one of the pack reeled and heeled as it was struck. In the conning tower they could hear the hollow boom of metal striking metal quite clearly. Brandt cursed as the U-boat came to a stop, already listing. He knew what would happen now. The rest would home in on the crippled boat.

He was right. The whole weight of the enemy attack fell on the other U-boat. The dawn was hideous with the snarl of engines, the howl of bombs, the banshee-like shriek of rockets, the bark and chatter of the flak.

A Thunderbolt was hit. Its pilot, blinded by escaping glycol, plummeted straight into the sea. Another one, roaring in at 300 mph, trailing black smoke behind it, smacked right into the side of another U-boat. It exploded in a blinding flash of angry red flame. The U-boat oil tank went up. A gigantic torch of flame raced across the U-boat deck like a great blowtorch. It swept all before it turning the deck crew into shrunken frozen pygmies in a matter of seconds.

Grimly Brandt looked around, feeling the old "phantom pain" in an arm that wasn't there. He frowned. One U-boat already gone under; another burning fiercely and sinking with the panic-stricken men in agony thrashing the water all around her. "Great crap on the Christmas tree!" he cursed at the sight and then, controlling himself he ordered, "Stand by to pick up survivors."

Degenhardt repeated the order into the voice tube and the U-boat changed course. The Luftwaffe fighters started to circle above them to give the U-boat protection.

Brandt told himself that the U-boat army had failed yet again. In a six-week fighting patrol the four of them had sunk exactly three Allied ships, perhaps a total of twenty thousand tons. For that they had paid with the loss of two U-boats and the lives of God knows how many young men. Yet somehow he always seemed to survive. No wonder the men called him "Lucky Bastard" Brandt behind his back. He knew full well that they fought and even offered good money to get into his crew before a combat patrol because they reasoned, in that superstitious way of sailors, that if they sailed with him they'd be safe.

Suddenly Brandt felt very old and weary. At the start of the war he had been a nineteen-year-old officer cadet, sailing with the likes of Prien, Kretmer and Cremer*. Now they had all vanished; dead, captured or beached. And he was twenty-five but felt more like two hundred and five. God, when would it all end? Wearily he rubbed his wooden arm as if trying to soothe the pain.

[* All famous U-boat aces.]

Two hours later the two surviving boats sailed into Kiel harbour, the black pennants signalling they had had "kills" fluttering from their conning towers, the crew — ragged, bearded and stinking — standing on their decks. At the dock the naval band played merrily. Dockers waved. Gold braided officers complete with swords and dirks saluted gravely. And the whores in their rabbit furs and too short dresses shrieked and waved their handkerchiefs.

Brandt watched without interest. He had seen it all before, too many times in fact. It was always the same: the hot bath, the shave, the drunken orgy and then the whores. Submariners never went to bed with decent girls any more. Their life was too short and brutal for that. It had to be paid women who would carry out any particular perversion they fancied — at a price. Then there'd be headaches, the shakes, the pox. Some senior desk-bound officer would read them a stern lecture, threatening this or that punishment to which they listened in bored disinterest. They knew by the law of averages they'd be dead before the year was out anyway. There'd be a round on the drill square with some old bastard of a drill sergeant yelling at them, "My God, what a bunch o' wet tails you really are. Now come on, put a bit o' frigging starch in it!" And then they'd be off again, probably to their deaths.

Suddenly Brandt snapped out of his gloomy thoughts. Grossadmiral Doenitz, the "Big Lion" as his U-boat crews called him, was striding across the wet dock towards the review stand. But it wasn't that which caught Brandt's attention. He had seen Doenitz often enough in this war. The "Big Lion" was very fond of his U-boat crews. It was the officer who towered above the admiral who attracted his notice.

He was a head higher than the Admiral and broad with it, shoulders like an ox, his face covered with duelling scars beneath the rakishly tilted SS cap with its gleaming silver skull and crossbones. "Skorzeny," he breathed out remembering the SS officer from the previous year's newsreels of the Mussolini rescue mission.

"What did you say, sir?" Degenhardt asked, looking up the skirt of one of the shrieking whores and noting with pleasure, and growing lust, that she was wearing no knickers.

"That officer there, next to the Big Lion. That's Otto Skorzeny."

Taking his eyes reluctantly off that delightful patch of black fuzz which indicated that the whore wasn't a true blonde, Degenhardt stared at the SS officer now mounting the review stand next to Doenitz. "Holy strawsack, sir," he exclaimed. "You're right! Wonder if they going transfer the lot to the armed SS?" He grinned.

Brandt grinned, too. "For all the good we're doing these days in the North Atlantic, Number One," he commented drily, "shouldn't be surprised if they do."

"U-boatmen, sailors, comrades," Doenitz's harsh rasping voice echoed and re-echoed around the bleak U-boat pens as he spoke into the microphone. "I welcome you back to the Homeland. You have done well. Folk, Fatherland and Fuhrer are proud of you."

He paused and gave them his steely eyed stare. Someone farted. They had heard it all before. They wanted nothing more than suds and gash. Heroic speeches were superfluous.

But Doenitz went on determinedly, "Your kills have not been as great as they used to be, comrades. The enemy has grown very powerful. But we have new weapons, terrible weapons, which the Fuhrer, in his infinite wisdom, has kept for this moment when our great country enters the final phase of this decisive struggle."

Brandt forgot Doenitz's speech. He had heard it, or something very like it, often enough in the place. The quayside at Kiel was peopled with ghosts for him, men who had stood at ease and listened to that same speech before departing, never to return. He noticed that Skorzeny, the big SS officer, seemed to be watching him. Why? he wondered. Were they really going to be beached now that the U-boat had lost its old effectiveness against the might of the

Allied navies and turned into infantry stubble-hoppers? Was Doenitz's speech leading up to that?

"Soon, comrades," Doenitz was saying heartily, fanatical blue eyes blazing, "we start taking the war to the enemy's homelands, just as we did in the glorious days of 1941 and 1942. Then we had the Tommies in particular almost on their knees and finished off till fate turned against us. This time there will be no help for them and their American allies. Providence is on our side now. We shall beat them. More I cannot tell you at this moment. It is a state secret." He gave them a wintry smile, his tight, thin lips moving as if on rusty springs. "But first, comrades, you must enjoy yourselves. You know what the seaman returning on leave always says to his sweetheart? I shall tell you: Look at the floor, beloved, because you'll be seeing the ceiling only for the next forty-eight hours." He laughed and dutifully the crew laughed with him in the hope that the Big Lion would pay for the night's orgy. He usually did.

Doenitz stiffened to attention and raised his bejewelled baton to his cap. "Sailors, comrades, U-boatmen, I salute you."

"Still gestanden!" Degenhardt yelled hoarsely.

The crews clicked to attention and Doenitz nodded his approval.

"Wegtreten!" Degenhardt ordered and with a rush the crews broke ranks, throwing their caps in the air, springing over the side of the boats without orders heading for the shrieking, waving whores while white-coated naval stewards pushed their way through the excited throng handing out bottles of beer and schnapps with the usual formula ready on their lips: "With the Big Lion's compliments, boys ... The whores are paid for ... Have a good time ... Slip one in for me, mate ..."

Brandt relaxed and rubbed his bearded chin. "Number One, off you go first. I'll see you in the officer's, mess later on."

Degenhardt relaxed and grinned, too. "I won't be sober," he warned, "and I'll probably not have my trousers on either, sir."

"If you do you'll be the only one of my rogues who has. Off you go now. I see the Big Lion is bearing down upon us." Degenhardt saluted and departed hastily.

Brandt saluted while Doenitz introduced Skorzeny and for a moment the two men stared at each other. Skorzeny took in the hard-faced naval officer's left hand clad in a leather glove and guessed that he had lost a hand, perhaps even an arm. Kapitanleutnant Brandt looked as tough and as durable as Doenitz had said he was. He made his decision. "I have the Grand Admiral's permission, Brandt," he said in his soft Viennese accent. "I'm afraid there'll be no leave for you. You are to come with me."

Nothing could surprise Brandt anymore, so he said quite curtly, *"Klar,* Obersturmbannfuhrer." Then: "And where?"

"Nordhausen in the Harz."

Brandt nodded and Doenitz, sensing better than the SS man the hollowness that afflicted so many of his old hares these days after they had seen so many of their comrades vanish at sea, said winningly, "I think, my dear Brandt, that Obersturmbannfuhrer Skorzeny will be able to show you something there that'll liven even your jaded appetite."

"I hope so, sir," Brandt said without enthusiasm.

Together they started for the Grand Admiral's car. They passed two excited young seamen with their trousers around their ankles, busy copulating with the whores while their red-faced drunken comrades cried, "Race him, Heinz ... come on, you're winning!"

Skorzeny shook his head and said, "They don't waste time your blue boys*, Herr Grossadmiral."

[* Nickname for the German sailor, equivalent to "Jack Tar".]

"Just letting off steam after six weeks at sea, Skorzeny," Doenitz said. "Eh, Brandt?"

But Kapitanleutnant Brandt did not answer. For suddenly he had a premonition. With the certainty of a vision he knew that this visit to Nordhausen would mean his death.

FOUR

Brandt smelled the camp even before he saw it. The big Mercedes was turning a corner that led to the underground factory in the Harz mountains when the stench assailed his nostrils. It was like the cloying stink he remembered as a boy when his father had taken him to visit the monkey house in Berlin's zoo. He gagged and said thickly to Skorzeny, "What in three devils' name is that awful stink?"

Skorzeny said, "You'll see in a moment, Kapitanleutnant."

They turned the corner. Up in front of them loomed the face of the mountain. Before it was a large open courtyard surrounded by barbed wire, with stork-legged towers containing guards armed with sub-machineguns on the platforms. Inside skeletal, half-naked figures, men and women, were squatting on the ground to defecate. Further on there were piles of what Brandt took at first to be birch logs but as the car came closer he saw were corpses. There was a curious pearly-white colour about the heaps of dead bodies, all naked, and skin was withered over the bones so it was hard to distinguish their sex.

Brandt stared at Skorzeny aghast as the Mercedes halted at the gate. "What in heaven's name is this place?" he croaked, holding his handkerchief against his nose on account of that appalling stench. "Who are these people?"

"Political undesirables, degenerates, Jews, Russians, foreigners," Skorzeny rapped, showing his pass to the sentry who stiffened to attention when he saw the letter signed by the Fuhrer himself. "People who have no importance."

"But they're dying ... dying on their feet!" Brandt stuttered as he saw what he took to be a woman sway and fall to the cobbles, moaning softly like a child who knows it can never be soothed.

"They are fed as long as they work. When they can work no longer they aren't fed. It is a matter of simple economics," Skorzeny said unfeelingly as the car started to move forward again. "These are hard times for the German people. We cannot feel sorry for them. The future of Germany comes first."

Brandt opened his mouth to speak but found himself unable to do so; the scene was too appalling. There were dead and dying everywhere, lying in their own filth, while guards in highly polished jackboots strode among them, slapping the sides of their boots with their riding crops, proud smiles on their faces, as if the dying wretches constantly reminded them of their own superiority.

The car rolled on towards a large tunnel which led directly into the heart of the mountain. Railway lines ran in and out. Men in immaculate white overalls, who were obviously German, were directing walking skeletons who staggered back and forth under heavy loads of metal or lugged great canisters of some sort of fuel or other. Whenever they faltered or threatened to drop their loads they were shouted at brutally or given a blow or kick. "Germany's most secret factory," Skorzeny said proudly as if it was his own work. "The weight of the whole enemy air gangsters' air force could never penetrate this place. It is one hundred percent bomb proof."

"What is it?" Brandt asked thickly, too numb from what he had just seen to be curious even. He knew there were concentration camps and he supposed that this was one. But he had never suspected that the camps were so dreadful as this. He had believed what the government and party had always said: the camps were for the work shy and politically unreliable. There they worked hard on simple rations. But that wasn't true. *These were death camps!*

"You shall see shortly," Skorzeny said. "Driver, I think this is as far as we can go by car."

The driver stopped and they got out and Brandt stared about him at the half a dozen huge corridors sliced by dozens of others. All were air-conditioned, he could feel that, and high above his head there were fluorescent lights running the length of the rock ceiling.

With Skorzeny in the lead they marched down the main corridor then turned off into one of the side passages, narrower now and without any of the wretches bearing their loads. On both sides there were white metal doors, all of which bore the legend, "Entrance Strictly Forbidden" and from which Brandt could hear the muted hum of machines.

Half way down two giant SS sentries were posted, both with sub-machineguns slung across their burly chests. They spotted Skorzeny and clicked to attention. But they were not intimidated by an officer they must have instantly recognised. Instead the bigger of the two demanded in a gruff voice, *"Dienstausweis,* Obersturmbannfuhrer," while the other man looked at the visitors intently, finger curled round the trigger of his Schmeisser.

The scarfaced giant produced his pass from the Fuhrer himself. The sentry nodded his understanding and opened the door to allow Skorzeny and Brandt to pass through.

They entered into a huge room which seemed never ending, crammed with electrical gadgets, watertanks, testing apparatus and a dozen other scientific items which Brandt could not vaguely recognise. Skorzeny hesitated for the first time. He, too, seemed confused by the long benches heaped with scientific equipment, which appeared to go on forever. "Professor von Gluck," he called as he threaded his way deeper into the laboratory. "Ah, there you are, Herr Professor!" He smiled thinly.

Brandt saw a fat man with a bald head dressed in a dirty white lab coat and riding breeches. At his feet knelt a pretty, dark-haired girl dressed in the same striped pyjama-like uniform that the other wretches wore. But unlike them, from what he could see of her legs and arms, Brandt judged this one was very well nourished. Indeed she was inclined to plumpness.

Hurriedly the Professor turned, hands fiddling with his flies, fat face flushed crimson. "Obersturmbannfuhrer Skorzeny," he said flustered, "you are a little early." He looked down at the plump girl who had been kneeling in front of him and who wore the yellow star of a Jew on her uniform and commanded, *"Allez vite,* Sarah ... *Ça suffit."*

The girl hurried away eyes averted as she passed the two visitors and the Professor, finished with his buttons now, said, "My lab assistant ... Something fell to the floor ... she was helping me."

Skorzeny looked at the fat professor coldly. "She is a Jewess?"

"Yes, Obersturmbannfuhrer, but a very gifted one. We need her talents. She is a graduate of Sorbonne and the Montpellier Marine —"

"Enough," Skorzeny cut him short while Brandt looked at the flustered professor with undisguised contempt. This was the real face of the Third Reich he realised for the first time: half starved wretches working as some kind of slaves while fat pigs like Professor von Gluck took their pleasure with their women because they had the power of life or death over them. This was the New Order which Hitler had boasted would change old decadent Europe and for which he had fought all these years. It was a bitter thought and he was glad when Skorzeny said, "All right, Herr Professor, what have you to show us?" adding eagerly, "and does it *work?*"

The fat professor beamed. "All our last tests have been successful. They have been virtually one hundred percent. *Kommen Sie.* I'll show you, gentlemen."

Waddling slightly, his fat buttocks trembling in the too tight breeches, the professor led the way down the long laboratory, right to the end where he came to a stop in front of a large glass tank, filled with dirty green water.

Brandt sucked his front teeth. At the bottom of the tank lay a model of the newest kind of U-boat complete with snorkel. A dim perception of why he had been brought to this remote factory buried beneath the Harz Mountains started to dawn upon him. "Everything's built to scale," he heard the professor saying, "and we can also simulate water pressure at the varying depths which could be used for firing the missile. It is not —"

"Please demonstrate," Skorzeny interrupted. Obviously he had taken a dislike to the fat scientist, too.

"Yes, of course. Immediately, Obersturmbannfuhrer." Von Gluck waddled to the control desk at the far end of the glass tank and switched on the current, beaming all over his fat ugly face as if suddenly he was very pleased with himself.

He pressed a button and the submarine started to rise slowly as he commented, "I'm taking her to a simulated depth of twenty metres below the surface." He pressed a third button. The water began to move back and forth in a series of miniature waves. "That approximates to a force-three sea running," he announced and beamed at them.

In spite of his dislike of the fat professor Brandt watched fascinated as the submarine rose slowly in the moving water and the scientist now took up a hand toggle. The submarine came to a stop and floated there, moving slightly with the current.

"Now, gentlemen, this is it," the scientist announced. He pressed one of the several buttons on the hand toggle. On the forward deck of the miniature submarine a hatch started to slide open while a gleaming white pointed tube-like object began to appear.

Brandt repressed a gasp. It was a rocket rather like the new revenge weapons which they had shown in the *Deutsche Wochenschau** recently bombarding London from the stratosphere. What the devil was going on?

Slowly, as the rocket emerged from the hatch, the scientist started to count off the seconds, fat face intent, finger hovering over the third switch.

Now the rocket was completely out. The professor pressed the last button. The rocket quivered. Next moment it detached itself from the submarine and pushed its way effortlessly out of the water, rising into the air before plunging back into the water some ten metres away.

Skorzeny clapped his hands with delight like a little child who had just witnessed a conjuror produce a white rabbit from his top hat and said, *"Grossartig,* Herr Professor. Excellent!" For the first time since he had surprised the professor with the Jewish girl he smiled at him.

The professor shrugged in mock modesty, "We have done what we could for Folk, Fatherland and Fuhrer, Obersturmbannfuhrer. And may I say that is the tenth successful launch in succession. A much better success rate that they achieved

* German cinema newsreel.

at the testing grounds at Peenemunde last year."

"The distance — the distance your model covered. What is the equivalent in kilometres?"

"Approximately thirty kilometres," the professor answered, "give or take a few hundred metres."

Skorzeny was obviously pleased. His smile broadened and he said, "Herr Professor, you have done good work. Now, fill me in with the statistics, please."

"Only too glad to do so." The professor sat on the edge of the control table dangling one fat booted leg as if he were back in his pre-war lecture room impressing his students. "We have reduced the length and width so the amount of high explosive has had to be lowered. Still, we can pack six tons of high explosive into it and from the depth you saw we can hit a target fairly accurately if we are guided to it, up to a range of thirty kilometres."

Brandt, listening to all the data, could keep silent no longer; his curiosity got the better of him. "Obersturmbannfuhrer," he snapped, "what *is* all this about, please?"

Skorzeny looked down at him amused, an evil grin on his scarred face. "Oh, I'd have thought you would have tumbled to it all by now. Why my dear fellow, you are going to be given the great honour of taking the war to the New World."

Brandt looked at Skorzeny as if he had just gone mad. "Taking the war to the New World?" he stuttered.

"Yes, in December you and your crews will begin to bombard New York with the V-2."

FIVE

Brandt couldn't sleep. He lay beneath the monstrously thick *Federdecke* in his bedroom in the little village inn, listening to the sound of the wind in the pines and the regular but muted sound of hammering coming from the underground works a good two kilometres away.

Skorzeny, the professor and he had talked on long after their evening meal, with a sentry guarding the door of the *Stube* and the waiter innkeeper ushered in and out, also under guard. "We cannot be too careful," Skorzeny had said. "Of course, these people in the village know what's being made in the Nordhausen factory. They can see the V-2s being taken away all the time. But that is all."

They had talked of ranges, depths, loads and a dozen different technical matters until Brandt's head had been ringing with details and he had excused himself saying he was still tired from his six-week combat mission. Thereafter he had heard the clink of glasses and the sound of female laughter coming from the *Gaststube* below his bedroom and had guessed the professor had ordered up some of the slave women for the two men's pleasure. Then all had been silent save for the crunch of the sentry's boots outside and the rhythmic creaking of bedsprings somewhere further down the corridor. Still he had been unable to sleep.

As fantastic as it had all sounded, still the daring plan had intrigued him. A flotilla of the latest U-boats from the Bloehm and Voss Yard, Hamburg, would sail across the Atlantic and be in position for Saturday 16 December, 1944, when the Fuhrer was to launch his great offensive against the Americans. Each U-boat would carry six of the adapted V-2 rockets and a merchantman flying under a Bolivian flag would be standing by carrying further missiles. Each of the missiles would have a specific target in the Greater New York City area and each submarine would launch the rockets in the space of one hour. "That would mean," Skorzeny had enthused earlier on, that the equivalent of a hundred tons or more of high explosive will strike the city. The Jews and the bankers will be frightened out of their decadent minds. They'll be pleading with their fellow Jew, Roosevelt, to start peace talks within the hour. That and the victorious attack of our troops on land will certainly turn the war in Germany's favour."

Now Brandt savoured the words. There were plenty of "if's" to the plan. The enemy air force would react well before the last missile had been launched and as they would be only thirty kilometres off shore and in shallow water to boot it would be hardly likely that they'd survive the enemy air attack. For the Wolf Pack it would be a suicide mission.

Besides, how would they programme their targets exactly? He knew from what he had already read about the V-2 attacks on London that they were pretty much a hit-and-miss weapon. For the plan to have the impact Skorzeny intended there had to be some means of targeting their objectives correctly. "Don't worry yourself about that now, Kapitanleutnant Brandt," Skorzeny had reassured him when he had raised the point. "That will also be taken care of in due course. You see," he had given Brandt that scarfaced smile of his, "we'll have everything under control."

Brandt rose and switched on the bedside table light. He shivered and slipped into his dressing gown, noting as always just how absurd his wooden arm looked hanging over the side of the bed. He walked to the tiny window. It was snowing softly outside — the first snow of the winter. The little houses with their timber balconies and wooden beams already had a covering on their roofs so that they looked like a scene from a pre-war Christmas card. He smiled a little sadly. It was hard to realise at that moment that Germany was at war; that enemy troops were fighting on her borders to east and west; and that inside the Reich itself some terrible things were being done to harmless civilians in the name of "final victory" as the Fuhrer always called it.

His lean pale face hardened. Did he want to sacrifice his life, which he was sure he would if he carried out the daring mission, for a country like the one Germany had become? Still, he was a German, a patriot, who felt he had a duty to all those of the U-boat Arm who had already died in action. Their memory had to be honoured, surely?

A soft tap on the door of his room broke into his reverie. Automatically he looked at the dial of his wristwatch. It was already after eleven. Who could be knocking at this time of the night in a village where they presumably rolled up the pavements as soon as it was dark and went to bed with the chickens, as the saying had it? *"Ja, bitte,"* he called softly.

The girl he had seen in the professor's lab that morning came in. She was clad in a shabby cloth coat complete with Star of David and there were flakes of snow on her dark hair.

"You?" he said in surprise.

"Yessir," she said softly, keeping her gaze lowered. "The professor noted that your light was on. He sent for me. I live in the outhouse," she added almost apologetically.

"But why? Why come to me?" he asked, his surprise growing.

She dropped her gaze again and said nothing.

There was a heavy silence broken only by the soft metallic tick of the old clock in the hall outside. "Oh, I see," he said breaking it. "You mean for *that?*" She nodded. He said, "Sit down, over there. Do you want a cigarette?" He reached over for his gold cigarette case which the Fuhrer had presented to him when he had won his Knight's Cross back in '42.

"Yes, please," she said hesitantly, as if it were some kind of a trap. "They er, you feed us well, the technicians, but we are not allowed cigarettes. Usually we pick up the ends and try to make one good one out of them."

She took the cigarette, smelled it and then looked surprised when he offered her a light as she sat there straight-backed on the edge of the chair.

"Why don't you run away?" he said after a while. "You're healthy, you look fit, not like the others, and you speak German perfectly."

"I was born in Cologne. My father sent me to study in France in 1933 as soon —" She didn't complete her explanation but Brandt knew what she meant: as soon as the National Socialists had come to power in that year. "Why don't I run away?" she echoed his question and shrugged, her pretty face under the dark curly hair suddenly angry. "Where should I go?"

"How do you mean?"

"There is nowhere I can go in Germany. I have no papers, no ration cards, no friends or family left. And I have this," she indicated the yellow star on her coat.

"Take it off and flee to France?"

"*France!* It was the French who sent us to this place in the beginning."

"French!"

"Yes. They rounded us all up in mid-'42 and then those of us who had technical skills finally were sent here." She shrugged. "Those without skills are probably long dead." She said the words without emotion, as if she were long used to death.

"So there is no place for you to go," he said a little lamely. Outside the wind had risen and the snowflakes were beating against the little window in a white fury. She nodded and puffed at her cigarette. "What can you do then?" he asked after a little while.

"What can I do, save pray that you will lose the war and that I survive long enough to be freed by the Allies." For the first time she looked him directly in the eyes and he could see a fierce temperament lurking behind that seemingly docile façade. God knows, he thought, how she must have been humiliated by Germans like Professor von Gluck over these last years. Yet her spirit had not been broken.

"You'll survive," he said, astonishing himself somewhat.

"How do you know?" she asked, her gaze still fixed intently on his face.

"I've seen those with the mark of death on their faces. It is not on your face."

She laughed hollowly, a strange sound in that little bedroom, with the snow beating against the window and making it rattle. "I could be dead tomorrow, just like that!" She snapped her fingers together. "The professor might get tired of me. I might make a botch of one of the experiments. I might get in the way of the commandant when he's in one of his bad moods, which is often. There are dozens of ways that I could fall into disfavour with you *Germans.*" She spat out the word as if it were dirty, "and then they would dispense with me with no more feeling that squashing out some filthy beetle underfoot."

Brandt was taken aback. Naked hate blazed from her dark eyes. She had been the humble victim for too long. Her real self had taken over for a few moments. "Here," he said, "calm down. Take a drink of this. I don't want to be the cause of your getting into trouble." He went over to his naval greatcoat and pulled out a flask. "Best French cognac." He unscrewed the cap and poured her a stiff measure. "It's damned cold in here anyway. So you have a good excuse."

She hesitated.

"Go on," he urged. "Let's not talk anymore about — well, you know what."

She lifted the silver cup, her eyes suddenly brimming with tears. "Thank you," she choked as she sipped the cognac. "No one has treated me like a human being ... for so long." She let the cup fall to the floor, her shoulders heaving like a heartbroken child.

His heart went out to her. With his one hand he pressed her shoulder saying gently, "Don't cry ... please, don't cry ... I didn't want to upset you."

Head still bent, the tears flowing down her cheeks, her hand sought and found his. She pressed it hard. "Thank you," she sobbed. "Oh, thank God. You're the first kind person I have met in years ... *Thank you.*"

Outside the wind howled and the snowflakes beat against the window as they froze there as if for eternity — two young people caught up in a great conflict which had made them enemies but which would soon make them lovers.

She sneaked out of his bedroom just after dawn. He didn't want Skorzeny to know that she had slept with him and Brandt guessed the professor wouldn't say anything; for she had told him everything about the professor. The fat scientist was completely impotent but he insisted on trying and trying again. Once he had actually begged her to help him with tears in his eyes, crying in despair, "Make it stand, Sarah, please and I will give you the world." To no avail. "But as long as I try he remains my protector," she had explained as they had lain there together under the heavy rumpled feather-bed. "Besides, I know his nasty little secret."

"The swine," he had cursed. "I would like to cure his problem for him once and for all, with a sharp razorblade!"

That had made her laugh and they had made love again with her astride his body her naked body lathered in sweat as she rode him until exhausted.

Now, as he lay in the rumpled bed with the winter sound of boots crunching across the fresh snow and an excited child crying, *"Mutti,* there's snow ... snow everywhere!" he thought of her and her plight. Gerda Kunstmann — for Sarah was a name given to all Jewesses by the Nazis and not her real name — wouldn't last long. He had seen that this night. She couldn't control herself all the time. Her spirit was unbroken and once she let go, they'd know and deal with her accordingly. And that he couldn't let happen.

"You're getting a conscience at last, old house," a hard cynical voice rasped at the back of his mind. "What about those passenger liners you sank back in '41 and '42? How do you know that they weren't filled with innocent women and kids?"

But he ignored that inner voice. Instead he told himself he had to do something and do something very soon before it was too late. But what?

It was Obersturmbannfuhrer Skorzeny, surprisingly enough, who put the plan almost ready-made into his head over breakfast that morning. The giant scarfaced SS officer looked bad. He had deep circles under his eyes and a bandage soaked in vinegar tied around his head as he slumped in the little panelled *Stube* of the village inn, the fire crackling merrily in the green-tiled oven in the corner. He was already drinking beer although it was only seven in the morning.

"Must have overdone it last night with that fat swine the professor," he moaned thickly. *"Himmel, Arsch and Wolkenbruch!* that homemade kirsch must have been one hundred percent proof alcohol. Real rotgut." He shuddered and took another delicate sip of the cool beer. "Good, let's forget it, Brandt. I have already had a movement order drawn up for you. You'll proceed from here to

Goslar. There a staff car will be waiting for you. They've even fitted it with snow chains so that you'll be able to get through."

"To where, Obersturmbannfuhrer?" Brandt asked, his mind racing electrically.

"To Frankfurt, of course," Skorzeny answered sourly. "At Frankfurt, there's a Condor already fuelled up and ready to fly as soon as the weather improves."

Brandt waited 'till Skorzeny took another delicate sip at his beer. The Condor was a four-engined long-range plane used mainly for reconnaissance over the North Atlantic. Why should a plane like that be waiting for him? But he didn't dwell on the matter. He knew he had found a way of getting Gerda out of Nordhausen.

"Where is it flying you, Brandt?" Skorzeny said finally and answered his own question immediately. "I shall tell you, Lorient in France, as you know well."

"I do, Obersturmbannfuhrer. But Lorient has been isolated behind enemy lines since September. If it weren't such a tough nut to crack the Allies would have taken it long ago. Why Lorient?"

Skorzeny gave him a pained smile. "All in due time, Brandt. All in due time." He waved his hand. The interview was over.

SIX

"Now it'll start to get hairy," the big blond pilot said with a grin. "Down there," he pointed out of the cockpit window. "They'll already know we're here. From here right across Belgium into France, the Amis will be on the alert, all of them straining to put one right up our arse ... if you'll forgive my French, Fraulein," he added for Gerda's benefit.

Muffled as she was in a fur-lined flying suit and ill at ease as she had been ever since Brandt had ordered her sharply to get into the staff car "and ask no questions", she smiled at the pilot wanly and said, "I've heard worse, Herr Oberleutnant."

He returned her smile and, pointed out of the window. "There you are. Just as I said. The first of the Ami swine!"

Brandt craned his neck. Far down below he could see three silver shapes glistening in the autumn sunshine, trailing white vapour trails, climbing towards them.

"Mustangs," the pilot identified the enemy planes. "Hope they don't have superchargers. Then we're sunk. All right, I'm going to climb. We'd better go on oxygen." He indicated the masks hanging from the console. "Put those on as soon as you feel your breathing's getting a bit of a problem."

Brandt nodded to Gerda to do so but for the time being he felt his breathing was quite normal. He supposed it was something to do with being submerged in the U-boats for so long when oxygen was short; the lungs adapted he guessed.

Slowly, the big four-engined plane started to rise while below them the American Mustangs continued to climb. He watched, fascinated, for a few moments, telling himself it all seemed unreal, not at all like the deadly cat-and-mouse game of the U-boat battle. Then he forgot the enemy and concentrated on his plan. By now Gerda would be missed, at least by the fat swine of a professor, but somehow he suspected that he wouldn't report her missing. He hoped so, for Skorzeny, drunken bully that he was, would soon put two and two together and conclude that "my official interpreter", as Brandt had introduced the girl to the driver of the staff car, was Gerda and on her way to Lorient. A signal was all that was needed and Gerda would be arrested as soon as she stepped off the plane.

He hoped that wouldn't happen. But what was he to do with Gerda once they reached Lorient? Knowing the U-boat base from the days when he had been permanently stationed there back in '42 he guessed it would be still full of Gestapo men and police informers, both French and German. U-boat bases were always full of such people, intent on rooting out those who might betray sailing times and details to the enemy. In the besieged French port, without papers or a ration card, Gerda would soon be discovered he told himself.

He looked across at her as she sat there on the little metal-and-leather seat, muffled in the shapeless overall, her pretty face hidden by the oxygen mask. But he could still see those dark expressive eyes of hers and the look in them revealed she was frightened, not of death, he knew she had lived with death on a daily basis for two years, but of the unknown.

"There's an uncertainty about having your freedom, Klaus," she had said hesitantly when he told her he was going to take her from the camp at Nordhausen. "Here we all know that one day it will happen to us. You know?" He had nodded. "But outside, *it* could and it couldn't — at any time. That's even more frightening I think." She lowered her gaze as if reluctant to say any more in case he felt she was ungrateful for his risking his life to save her.

"I am determined to get you through," he replied. "I don't know how exactly at this moment. But somehow I will."

Now he thought of those bold words and wondered how he was going to keep that promise made at Nordhausen, with the dead and dying wretches lying in the freezing mud and dirty snow all around.

"Shitting optimists!" the pilot yelled above the roar of the engines, breaking into his thoughts. "Look at them!"

Again Brandt peered through the cockpit window. Bright white tracer was sailing through the clear air like glowing golf balls but falling well below the big Condor, as the four-engined plane continued to climb higher.

"They'll try flak next," the pilot bellowed, reaching for his oxygen mask, his face and lips already beginning to turn blue due to a lack of oxygen. "But I don't think they can be too accurate at this height ... Better put your mask on, Herr Kapitanleutnant."

Brandt nodded his understanding and reached for his own mask. Already his ears were beginning to pop and he felt a little light-headed as they did in the U-boats when the air started to run out.

Thus they flew on over the Belgium-French border, leaving the Mustangs behind, heading ever westwards.

"Metz," the pilot's voice came over the intercom, metallic and distorted. "Can you see, Herr Kapitanleutnant? Still under siege by the Amis."

Brandt could see the faint whiffs of smoke from the cannon and to the west of the city where the hills started a pall of black smoke was rising to the sky. He shook his head in mock wonder. His grandfather had been killed in the battle for Metz back in 1870 and his father had been wounded not far from the French city in 1918. Now they were still fighting for Metz.

He looked at Gerda and she looked back. Instinctively he knew what she was thinking: the world was crazy. Men were still fighting each other because they had been told to. From up here it all seemed pointless, a game with a lethal outcome played by insignificant creatures of no importance.

"We're going over another Ami air base," the pilot said pointing to the left. "Etain. Stationed there myself back in '40." His eyes sparkled at the memory. "Lived like God in France, as the saying goes. Holy strawsack, the wine and the women. You could have —" He stopped short, his eyes above the mask suddenly very serious. "Bandits at two o'clock. Gunner prepare for the works."

Brandt pressed his throat mike. "Where's the fire? They can't reach us, can they? We're too high."

"They can't reach us in height," the pilot agreed looking at some two-engined planes now climbing into the sky from the airfield below. "But if they're armed with what I think they're armed with, well, say good night and make a beautiful corpse."

"What do you mean?"

"They're Ami Mitchell medium-bombers and some of the latter models have been armed with a nasty 75 mm cannon."

"Oh, my God," Brandt exclaimed, "that's bigger than the cannon we had on my last U-boat!"

"Exactly. If one of those boys get in range of us —" He didn't finish his sentence but Brandt knew what he meant. The 75 mm cannon had a range of well up to a kilometre and a half.

Up in his turret the gunner had opened fire. There was the stink of burned cordite. Even with the engines roaring as the Condor tried to climb even higher Brandt could hear the clatter of the empty cartridge cases falling to the metal floor. Brandt looked across at Gerda. She was frightened, he could see that.

Suddenly the plane reeled. "Christ on a crutch!" the pilot cursed. He grabbed a tighter hold on the stick as the plane's nose tipped. Sweat standing out in opaque beads on his forehead, eyes bulging like those of a madman, he fought to keep the plane in the air.

Brandt peered out of the window. The two Mitchells were climbing steeply. Puffs of smoke enclosing violet flame came from their noses as the gunners fired their cannon upwards. Now the Condor was flying through flame and explosions on both sides. It rocked and juddered. Instruments shattered and glass tinkled to the deck. Brandt swallowed hard. It was just like being in a U-boat during a depth charge attack, and worse.

"Got the shitehawk!" the gunner's excited cry came over the intercom in triumph.

One of the Mitchells had been hit by his tracer. Smoke was pouring from its starboard engine and it had started to veer to the left as if it intended to land back on the field. But still the other one pressed home its attack, its big nose cannon thudding away.

At the controls the blond pilot cursed, the veins standing out at his neck with the strain as he willed the Condor to rise ever further and get out of range. But that wasn't to be. Suddenly the plane was struck a hammerblow on the side like a punch from a giant fist.

Gerda screamed into her mask as a great ragged hole appeared in the fuselage and an icy wind rushed in.

"Grosse Kacke am Christhaum!" the pilot cursed as the plane went into a dive, flames already licking greedily at the two port engines. "The shitting petrol lines have been ruptured!" Desperately he fought to control the crippled plane.

Now they were coming down fast. Brandt whipped off his oxygen mask. Gerda did the same. "Don't worry," he yelled above the howl of the wind, "everything will be all right!"

"All shitting wrong," the pilot yelled, as Brandt tore off his mask for him. "Come on, you whore's son, answer ... answer, damn you!" With all his strength he heaved at the controls.

But the Condor was refusing to answer. The ground was racing to meet them at an alarming rate. Still the pilot fought on as the victorious Mitchell continued to blast away, pumping shell after shell at the big four-engined plane.

They were hit again. Over the intercom the gunner screamed, "I can't see, skipper ... honest, I can't see. I'm blind. Blind!"

"For Chrissake, shut up!" the pilot screamed, his face crimson and lathered in sweat as if it had been greased, "Can't you un —" The plane yawed frighteningly.

"Parachutes?" Brandt yelled.

"Too low!" the pilot yelled back. "Stand by. I'm going to try to ditch in that lake over there. Take the impact better." He lowered the undercarriage even as he spoke in an attempt to reduce his speed.

Brandt flashed a look out of the cockpit. They were barely a hundred metres above the ground now. It was rushing below them at a tremendous rate. In some fields to their left men in khaki uniforms were shooting at the speeding plane with their rifles. Beyond them lay a lake fringed with large trees. God, Brandt told himself, if we hit one of those we'll be done for! "Hold your head down and cover it with your arms," he yelled at Gerda. "Keep your feet off the floor, too. We're —"

He broke off as the pilot with one last supreme effort pulled the dying plane up a little just as it seemed about to smash into a group of skeletal oaks. But the undercarriage went. He could hear the rending, tearing sound of metal being ripped off by the tops of the trees.

Next moment they slapped into the water. For a moment they were blinded by the flurry of angry green water. Then they were careening on crazily, their progress slowing though. A metal object, a kind of tall pole perhaps used for tethering boats, loomed up. The pilot tried to avoid it to no avail. They slammed right into it. The perspex of the cockpit shattered into a glistening spider's web. The pilot screamed shrilly, hysterically, like a woman. The shaft of the wheel had gone clean through the centre of his face. He slumped there with the metal protruding from the back of his head, dead.

Brandt felt something smack him hard in the nose. Blood jetted from his nostrils. For a moment he thought he was going to black out. He saw stars, a brilliant silver, exploding before his gaze. Brandt shook his head hard. Everything swum back into focus; the dead pilot, the shattered cockpit, the plane, its wings ripped, sinking slowly into the green slimy water.

"Gerda, come on," he cried. "Let's get out of here, *quick!*"

She didn't move. A thin trickle of blood wound its way down from her left nostril

"Gerda!" he cried as the surviving crew members started to force open the hatch which was already partially submerged in water.

She shook her head. "I'm all right, Klaus," she said a little weakly. He tugged her belt free and pulled her to her feet. "We're going," he cried above the crackle of flames from the rear of the shattered plane. He shoved and threw his weight with the others against the hatch. With a harsh metallic rending sound it gave and all of them found themselves up to their knees in water.

Brandt flung a glance outside. Some half a kilometre away armed figures were running towards the stranded plane. He drew his pistol and fired a few wild shots in their direction. They went to ground immediately, as he had hoped they would.

"Scatter," he yelled at the survivors, "We're dead if we group!" He grabbed Gerda's hand and dragged her out of the sinking plane. "Come on ... I think we can wade ashore."

Minutes later they were running for their lives.

TWO

BRANDT

SEVEN

Lt Commander Ian Fleming lounged against the great white mantelpiece of Room 39 and waited till the creaking old porter had built up the coal fire. It was a freezing autumn morning. When the porter had limped out talking to himself, as it seemed to the tall good-looking commander that all the porters did at the Admiralty, he said: "Did you see last night's report, sir?"

The Admiral took his cigarette out of his mouth and said, "Yes, I saw it, Ian. What about it?" He turned his gaze back to the barrage balloons tethered above Horse Guards Parade like silver sluggish elephants.

"Well, sir," Fleming said carefully. "What are the Boche up to running E-boats into Lorient at this late stage of the game?"

The Admiral shrugged. Privately he thought the former *Times* correspondent was too big for his boots. "Search me?"

Fleming ignored the remark. "Sir," he said firmly, "I have a theory."

"You usually do. All right, tell me."

Outside the sirens started to wail once more. Probably flying bombs spotted off the east coast, the admiral told himself. He could cope with the doodle-bugs but those bloody V-2s coming straight out of the stratosphere without warning, well, that was another bloody kettle of fish altogether. In the corridor one of the ancient porters was saying in a low voice, as befitted that august place, "Gentlemen, please, the air-raid warning is being sounded. Would you please repair to the shelters in the basement ... gentlemen, the air-raid warning is being ..." Both the Admiral and Fleming ignored the appeal. Only civilians and Wrens went into the shelters. To the east the anti-aircraft guns started to thunder.

"Now, why are the Jerries risking their precious E-boats to run into Lorient? It has long been evacuated as a submarine base? The U-boats cleared out once the Yanks had surrounded the place. Now Lorient is effectively a prison camp for the remaining Jerries there. So —" He paused. There was that sinister putt-putt of a flying bomb. Automatically the two of them turned their heads.

Sailing right across London came the German bomb, one ton of high explosive powered by what appeared to be a two stroke motor. A clipped winged Spitfire was in pursuit and both men knew what the pilot was intending to do.

"Damned fool, must be a damned Pole," the Admiral exploded. "They're all mad. He's trying to tip the wing of the bloody thing and send it down over Central London."

He stopped short. The V-1's engine had cut out. Instinctively Fleming placed his hands in front of his genitals. One never knew and he was not intending to lose the family jewels to any damned Jerry wonder weapon. The V-1 went into a steep dive. There was an almighty crash. The windows rattled and flapped. A pall of smoke started to rise about half a mile away.

"You were saying," the Admiral said as if nothing had happened.

Fleming removed his hands quickly. He hoped the Admiral hadn't seen the gesture but he had for he said, "Don't worry about 'em, Ian. When you get to be my age you'll be quite philosophical about the whole messy business in bed."

Fleming grinned. "Haven't reached that stage yet, sir. Besides, I've got a date tonight with a rather liberal Wren officer. Well, sir as I was saying, the Boche are running E-boats into Lorient. The question is, what are they carrying?"

"You're going to tell me so get on with it, Ian," the Admiral replied in his usual bluff no-nonsense manner.

"My little nancy boy has come up with some quite interesting details."

Back in 1942 when Fleming, then a lieutenant, had first suggested using French homosexuals as agents in Occupied French ports, Admiral Godfrey, his then boss, had exploded. "Do you mean to say, Ian, that you're going to get a lot of Frog pansy boys to spy for Naval Intelligence?"

"Naturally, sir," Fleming had replied as if it was the most obvious thing in the world. "Where there are sailors there are nancy boys — bits of the other as the ratings call it. Always has been like that."

The Admiral sniffed and said, "For an officer who only joined the Royal Navy three years ago you seem to know a damned lot about the ways of sailors, bent or otherwise."

"Well, sir, didn't Old Winnie himself say once, forget where, that the Royal Navy in the old days was renowned for 'the lash, rum and buggery'?"

"Touché," the Admiral had conceded.

"So, sir, we use the jolly old bum boys to pump the Boche sailors. I mean who would suspect a mincing nancy boy with painted fingernails of being a spy. Much too soft."

Thus, back in 1942 the "Fleming Riseau" as it was called in Room 39 had come into existence, using volunteer homosexuals and later women prostitutes to obtain the information on German naval movements which Room 39 so badly needed.

"Well," the Admiral demanded as the sound and rumble of the anti-aircraft guns came closer and closer as the gunners chased the V-1s across the London skyline. "What have your tame Frog nancy boys come up with on these E-boats?"

"Lots of bits and pieces. They could mean something significant," Fleming frowned, "and then again they could mean nothing. They are certainly interesting odds and sods but they could be mere boasting and shooting a line. You know what matelots are like, sir, British or Boche."

"Get on with it, Ian. That's what we're paid for here in Room 39, to put the bits and pieces together and make sense of the jigsaw. Fire away."

"Well, one thing for sure is that the E-boats are bringing in bits and pieces of the latest subs and something else which our chaps haven't made out yet."

Fleming saw he had caught the Admiral's interest for the latter said, "That is indeed strange. We've got them pretty well bottled up in the Baltic now," he meant the enemy U-boats. "Once the codebreakers at Bletchley give Coastal Command the wire they're on to the Jerries like a shot as they try to pass through the straits of the Kattegat."

"I know, sir," Fleming said. "We knocked out two of Brandt's Wolf Pack only the other week." Like all the other officers in Naval Intelligence, Fleming knew the names of the key enemy submarine skippers by now — those who had survived.

"It could be that they are really making an attempt to open up Lorient again. The RAF boys of Bomber Harris haven't been able to crack the sub pens and it's easier to slip into the Atlantic from there. That could be it Ian."

"I thought the same, sir. But there's another thing, too. One of my, er, Frog nancy boys has taken up with a German lieutenant. According to the agent, Paul, the Jerry's highly chuffed because he says he's going on a secret mission soon. Apparently the Jerry dresses in civvies most of the time *and* speaks English."

The Admiral frowned. "English, that's a bit odd, Ian. Well, go on."

"This is the clincher, sir. According to Paul, his lover tells him he is to go on this mission, whatever it is, by submarine."

The Admiral could not conceal his surprise. "By submarine!" he echoed. "That is strange: an army officer, as queer as a fruitcake, going on a secret mission by submarine. Now, I wonder what his little game is?"

Fleming didn't answer. Instead he leaned against the elegant white mantelpiece and lit one of those expensive cigarettes which he had specially made for him at a little shop on Bond Street. Mentally he recorded the look on the Admiral's face, the flying bomb putt-putting by the window outside, the fat barrage balloon sagging in the windless sky. It was his mental picture of the moment, a still life dated autumn 1944. After the war, when he began to write, he knew such scenes would be useful.

"Well, what do you make of it, Ian?" The Admiral's voice shook a little as yet another doodle-bug exploded outside and rattled the tall windows of Room 39.

"Can't say exactly, sir. The German lieutenant chap could be a spy intended for the UK. I mean they have landed them here before in the early part of the war."

"But they'd hardly go to the bother of re-building subs with the parts brought by the E-boats to transport one spy to the UK, would they? Not at this stage of the war at least."

Fleming frowned. "I suppose you're right. And there's one other thing. According to Paul there are more of these chaps, mostly wearing civvies but sometimes uniform. There seems to be a couple of small hotels in the old port where they're quartered."

Now it was the Admiral's turn to frown. Outside the last of the V-1s had gone and already the sirens were beginning to sound the all clear. Fleming wondered for how long. The enemy was firing the damned things, probably from Holland now, all day long.

"I've fought the Hun in two wars, Ian," the Admiral finally broke the silence. "I don't trust him. Just when we think he's beat he pulls a surprise out of the hat, giving us a ruddy great shock. He did so in March '18 with that great push which nearly flung us back into the Channel, just when we thought we'd got him licked. Look how he's defending the Siegfried Line at the moment. Knocks back everything the Yanks can throw at him. Why, if he's done?" The Admiral shook his head. "Something stinks somewhere, Ian. The old Hun is up to something."

"What are your orders, sir?" Fleming asked smartly.

"Oh, come off it, Ian. You sound like something out of the *Boys' Own Paper* begad. But we do need more information. Get those nancy boys and whores you employ in Lorient to find out some more, toot sweet."

"It could be dangerous for them, sir. Paul says the Gestapo's very keen in Lorient."

The Admiral looked at him as if he wasn't quite right in the head. "They're only pansies and whores after all, Ian. Who gives a shit about that breed? You can't make an omelette without cracking eggs, you know." He slapped his heavily braided cap on the side of his head at a rakish angle saying, "I'm off to White's for a drink. See to it, Ian, be a good chap." Pulling on his elegant leather gloves he chanted, "When the Earl pulled out his bloody great tool at tea ... to do the page wrong ... His chaplain cried in incredulity ... How long! O Lord, how long!" He winked cheerfully at Fleming and swaggered out, leaving the latter to ponder mightily at the strangeness of senior regular naval officers.

But not for long. Vain and arrogant as he was, Fleming was also a resourceful, keen, hard-working intelligence officer. He knew he was on to something at Lorient. The Admiral's own feelings that something strange was going on in the Breton port confirmed his own. He knew that he was putting his agents' lives at more risk by pressing them to find out more details of what was happening over there, but that was a chance they'd have to take. As the Admiral had just said, you couldn't make an omelette without cracking eggs.

He made up his mind and, leaving the office, headed for the great wireless signals' room which lay in the basement. He had not signalled direct to any of his agents inside the besieged port for a long time. But he had Josette who lived just outside the port and who, with the help of the Americans besieging the place, could pass through their lines and those of the Germans — the latter were bribed — to sell her farming wares on the black market. He would direct her to contact Paul and order him to find out more.

He passed a Wren bending over a desk showing a delightful rump and a stretch of tantalising black silk stocking. For a moment he was tempted to give that delicious bottom a good wallop. But he resisted the temptation. It would, after all, be conduct unbecoming for an officer and gentleman. "Well, Ian, old boy, you're an officer," he told himself cheerfully, "but definitely no gentleman as far as women are concerned."

Moments later he was in the coding room having his signal to Josette in France coded and wondering yet once again what the hell was going on in Lorient.

EIGHT

Each step was agony, sheer unadulterated agony. The snow came down in sheets. Brandt could see no more than a couple of metres down the cobbled French country road. Behind him, protected a little by his lean tall body, Gerda trudged along up to her ankles in snow as the wind raged and whipped the icy flakes against her livid, frozen face.

At first Brandt had thought this sudden snowstorm a blessing. It had stopped dead the chase by the Ami soldiers. He had told himself that only a fool, or a fugitive, would venture out on a day like this. It had helped, too, that the survivors had broken up, some heading for cover, others slinking away because they didn't want to be held up by the girl and her one-armed companion. Now the two of them were alone in this raging white, whirling world.

Brandt reckoned that they were somewhere near the site of the greatest battle of the first World War. He had been there to visit back in '40, that year of victory, and he recalled how the road had begun to rise from the Plain of Woevre towards the wooded heights on which the battle had been fought. Beyond lay the River Meuse and the city of Verdun itself. Now the road was beginning to rise.

He turned and, bellowing at the top of his voice, told Gerda where he thought they were. "There are still ruined villages up there. I think we'll be able to find shelter at least. Are you all right?"

"Of course," she answered, teeth chattering. "Just let's keep going."

"Agreed." He knew what she meant. If they stopped now God knows whether they'd be able to start again.

So they slogged on over that snow-engulfed road, fighting the pitiless, snow-laden wind, forced onwards and onwards by sheer naked willpower. By two o'clock on that terrible afternoon Brandt told himself they were on the right route. Barely glimpsed through the flying snow he saw the stone road sign with its helmet on top of it. It was the "Sacred Way" as the French called it: the sole road available to the French in 1916 to bring up supplies for their troops fighting on the heights. Wearily he went over to it and wiped away the snow. He read VERDUN 3 KILOMETRES"

Without wasting any more energy he tugged Gerda's arm. "Into the woods," he ordered. "We're here ... and the firs will give us some protection against this blasted wind."

Gratefully she nodded her head and they blundered up the slope at the side of the road into the trees, feeling the force of that dreadful storm lessen almost immediately.

There were stretches of rusting barbed wire, trenches, shell holes everywhere and they had to be very careful as they threaded their way through the stunted firs, peering through the snow for the first sign of shelter. While they did so Brandt wondered about the girl. Obviously he couldn't attempt to take her with him to Lorient. Then he told himself the clock would really be in the pisspot. Skorzeny would tumble to what had happened straight away. But the girl seemed to have no inclination to stay in France. Indeed she hated those who had first arrested her and sent her to the camps. But dare he let Gerda approach the Amis? If they started interrogating her they'd soon figure out what was going on and he couldn't risk that. But what was he going to do with her?

"Klaus," her urgent voice broke into his thoughts.

"What is it?"

"Over there," she pointed to the left. "There's a light ... I think."

He screwed up his eyes against the whirling snow. For a moment he couldn't see anything and was just about to tell her that she was imagining things when he spotted it himself: a thin yellow light which wavered a little as if affected by the wind.

"Come on," he said, new hope in his voice. "Let's have a look." As he spoke he fumbled underneath his flying overall and tugged out his little service pistol, just in case.

The place was a grey stone construction typical of the area, complete with yellowing tobacco leaves hanging from under the eaves with a huge pile of snow covered logs just outside the door; and it was inhabited all right. There was a yellow paraffin lamp in the dirty window and wood smoke poured from the chimney.

Gerda wiped the wet snow from her pretty face and asked anxiously, "What will we do? You know I don't trust the French after ..."

"We must chance it," he cut her short in a harsh whisper. "We've got to get out of this snow and find some warmth. Leave it to me."

He crept forward in the snow, face set and determined. The storm howling all about deadened the sound of his feet on the snow. Not altogether. From the lean-to shed attached to the cottage there was the sudden rattle of a chain. He started. Under his breath he cursed, there was a damned hound in there. He'd have to chance it. The beast would begin barking at any minute. He gripped the door handle and took a deep breath. "Here goes!" he commanded himself. He forced it open.

An old crone in a man's cap shot up from her chair in front of the red-hot pot-bellied stove. Her hand, scraggy and freckled, flew to her wrinkled neck. She was obviously terrified by this strange apparition which had appeared so startlingly out of the storm. Her thin lips trembled violently and saliva trickled out of the side of her toothless mouth.

Brandt jerked his pistol up at her and snapped, *"Ou sent les autres?"* He flashed a look around the poverty-stricken place, furnished with a few sticks of ancient furniture.

She continued to tremble unable to get out a word.

Brandt strode across the room and opened the only other door. A great sagging brass bed filled the place, underneath it a chamberpot which hadn't been emptied yet. But the bedroom was empty. He waited no longer. Keeping his eyes fixed on the old crone he called through the open door, "Gerda, come in, quick. There's only an old woman here."

Suddenly he saw by the look in the old woman's rheumy eyes that she had understood him. She had understood German. "All right," he commanded in his native language, "you can sit down again. But be careful. No tricks." Obediently she did so as Gerda staggered through the door out of the flying snow and leaned weakly against the wall.

"Thank God," she gasped weakly. "Thank God." Next moment she slumped to the floor completely exhausted.

Hurriedly Brandt gathered her up and lifted her to the fire. To the old crone he said, "Something hot ... something hot to drink. Quick!"

"Wird gemacht," she quavered in the thick accent of Lorraine, and suddenly Brandt remembered that this had been the linguistic border between French and German speakers up to 1918. She had probably spoken German till that time as her native language and had been forced when the French had taken over to speak their language.

Ten minutes later Gerda had revived. Now she drank a steaming milky coffee in front of the glowing stove, the colour back in her cheeks, while the old crone was frying potatoes and eggs on top of it, filling the pathetic little shack with an odour of good food that made Brandt almost ready to drool.

For a while they listened to the old woman as she explained to him that she had fled here when Metz, her hometown, had been surrounded. There were many such as she living in the abandoned ruined villages of the battlefield and the great underground caves which both sides had hollowed out of the chalk during the great battle. The French, she said, left them alone and they survived by bartering what eggs their chickens laid with the Americans who garrisoned the *Maginot Casern* down in the city below.

"Are there many Amis in the town?" he asked.

"Not many," she answered. "They are at the front. But plenty of French, a pack of whoremongers and pimps." She spat at the stove and the spittle hissed and sizzled. The two of them grinned. The old woman obviously didn't like her fellow citizens.

Carefully Brandt asked. "There is a railway station in Verdun, isn't there?" For slowly a means of escape was beginning to form in his mind. She nodded and he said, "Is it heavily guarded by the French?"

"Yes," she answered, "but it doesn't matter, *Herr.* As long as you have this," she made a gesture as if counting money with her dirty fingers, "none of that lot will give you trouble. Hitler himself could get through them as long as he had the money."

Brandt laughed shortly and then said, "Old woman, I think it is time for you to retire to your bed for a while. I shall talk to you again later."

She looked at him suspiciously. "You're not going to do anything to me?" she asked a little fearfully.

"No, mother. I just want to be alone with my fiancée."

Her scraggy old face looked suddenly very lecherous. "You can have my bed for that if you like."

Brandt laughed a little hollowly. "I'm afraid we're a bit too done in for that. Thank you for the offer, though."

"Suit yourself," the crone answered and shuffled into the bedroom and closed the door behind her.

"Think of the fleas," Brandt said and smiled down at her.

Gerda pressed his hand, eyes full of love. "I wouldn't mind, for you."

"Listen," he changed the subject. "We've got to get out of here. As soon as this snowstorm stops they'll be on the lookout for us."

"What shall we do? We have no French papers, nothing."

He slapped his inside pocket. "But we have French money, plenty of it. If the French are as venial as the old crone makes out —"

"They are," she said with sudden bitterness.

He ignored the interruption. "Then we shall buy and bribe our way out."

"How?"

"By train, from down there in Verdun. You shall go via Dijon, Lyons and then to where you came from, Montpellier. All those places have been captured by the Amis and the French. You're safe from the ... er us ... there."

She didn't look convinced. She said, "And then what do you think I should do?"

"Cross into Spain. Scores of our deserters did it during the Occupation and plenty of Allied escapers as well. With money I'm sure you'd easily find a guide."

"And you?" She placed her hand on his knees as if he was about to go and she was sub-consciously restraining him.

Brandt looked suddenly grim. "I have my duty."

"But Germany has lost the war. Why go on? You ... we ..." Suddenly she looked very vulnerable, hurt.

"I think so, too," he said simply and stroked her hair with his good hand. "But I can't be a rat and desert the sinking ship now. But when it's all over and you could wait —"

"Of course I could!" she said urgently, her face transformed abruptly. She pressed her cheek against his arm. "For you who have been so kind to me, the only person to be kind to me in years, yes, how I could wait!"

"We must work out a plan. How we shall remain in contact, come what may. Then we'll leave this damned continent. I'm sick of it. Europe is decadent, degenerate, worn out —" He stopped short.

Slowly, one by one, she was opening his fly buttons. "What?" he said.

"Shush," she whispered tenderly. "Let's not plan now. Let us just feel."

She placed both her hands inside his trousers. She cupped his organ as if it were something very precious. She opened her mouth to receive him. She used her tongue with a long stroking motion, first on the underside, then around the tip. He grew larger, groaning softly with pleasure. She repeated the long stroking motion. She stopped. He waited tensely, his heart beating furiously. Passionately she pressed tight at the tip once more and then opening her mouth wider allowed the whole length to slide in.

He was unable to contain himself any longer. He cried out with the sheer pleasure of it all. She felt the spasms as he convulsed and with her free hand she patted his leg gently as if comforting him. "Gerda ... Oh, Gerda!" he said huskily, panting as if he had just run a great race. "Gerda ..."

Outside the snow still beat against the dirty little window. They lay there as if frozen for all eternity, two lost souls caught up in a great conflict which ruled their lives in all its awesome cruelty.

Half an hour later when they heard the old crone stirring in the squeaky bed in the tiny bedroom they roused themselves. It was beginning to stop snowing. Soon, Brandt knew, they would have to go.

NINE

"Adieux la vie, adieu l'amour, adieu toutes les femmes ... car nous sommes tous condamnés ... nous sommes les sacrifiés ..." The French recruits chanted miserably as they struggled out of Verdun station, lugging their bags made of old carpets and chivvied by NCOs who looked bored and had cigarettes seemingly glued to their bottom lips, even when they shouted orders.

"No good," the old woman croaked as she limped at their side, carrying the precious eggs which Brandt's money had just bought on the black market in front of the Hôtel Cog Hardi. "Scum ... all French soldiers are scum." She hawked and spat in the yellow stained slush.

"Be quiet, old woman," Brandt hissed. "We don't want to attract any attention." Now he was dressed in a shabby suit, again bought in front of the Coq Hardi on the black market but he still did not have papers and he guessed that the gendarmes or the military police would ask for some form of identification at the station barrier.

With his wooden arm they would see that he wasn't a deserter or someone attempting to avoid compulsory military service. Still, he didn't possess valid papers.

They entered the big gloomy station filled with recruits for the Verdun garrison being watched by blue-coated gendarmes in pairs, with stony faces and their hands resting on their pistols. There were Americans, too, looking equally bored but infinitely better fed. They, too, were being watched by their own military police, giants all in white-painted helmets and carrying long white clubs. There were even a few prostitutes shivering in the shadows in their rabbit-skin coats and too short floral dresses. But no one seemed interested, not even the rich GIs. Perhaps it was too cold.

Brandt nodded to Gerda. She nodded back and walked over to the ticket counter as they had rehearsed while he remained behind with the old crone.

There was a long line of civilians waiting for tickets and he used the time to survey the barriers beyond. There were the usual ticket collectors stamping their feet in the cold and clicking their clippers as if eager to start operating. And each barrier had its own two cops, one French and one American. They would be the ones on the lookout for deserters and men without passes.

"Don't worry, my lad," the old crone said encouragingly, for ever since he had given her the small fortune of one thousand francs that morning she had become very friendly. "They're all fools. And if they aren't you'll just grease their palms."

He nodded and wished she would shut up, for she was speaking in her German Lorraine dialect. He bit his lip. Gerda was almost up to the window now. She spoke to the official. Brandt waited, tensed and anxious, but nothing happened. The clerk handed her the tickets and in moments she was back at his side, saying a little breathlessly, "No problem. I even got us two reserved seats. The tip," she winked, "helped."

"All right, mother" Brandt said to the old crone. "Remember what I told you back in your place."

"I know ... I know," she cackled. "I may be old but I'm not a fool. Come on, my darling son, let us go." She pressed closer to him and his nostrils flared in disgust. God how she smelled of sweat, garlic and urine!

Together they started to move to the barrier. To their left the door of the station bar opened. For a moment the platform was submerged in loud raucous noise from the whores inside and the swift tinny accordion music of a radio playing a java. But Brandt did not seem to hear it. His eyes were fixed almost hypnotically on the two officials at the barrier: the American, big, bored, with his belly bulging underneath his "Ike" jacket; and the Frenchman, lean, middle-aged, with the ribbons of the old war on his tunic. His eyes were mean and permanently suspicious of everyone, as if he had been a policeman for a long time. To Brandt that gaze meant trouble. With his good hand he felt in his pocket for his pistol.

They came ever closer. A train came chugging in. Steam flooded the platform. Its great steel wheels gave one final clatter then the locomotive groaned to a stop as if exhausted. Doors were flung open, pale-faced worried recruits came tumbling out clutching their carpetbags. NCOs' whistles shrilled. Somebody yelled an angry order. The recruits shuffled into some semblance of a formation. The barriers were opened wider to let them out. A little ferret of an NCO stamped to the head of the group. Over his shoulder he yelled an order almost angrily.

The formation lurched into movement, the recruits out of step, faces resigned to what was to come. Brandt nodded to Gerda. She understood: this was the best opportunity to get through the barrier. They quickened their pace. The crone protested. They ignored her. Now the recruits were shuffling by them: the look on their faces said: "We're cannon fodder. We know it. *Fuck off!*"

They came up to the barrier. The big American GI chewed gum. He looked bored as he stared into nothing, waiting for his shift to come to an end so that he could sink a few beers and head for his local shack-up job. Not the French gendarme: his eyes were everywhere, taking in the recruits, the people loitering on the platform, the people approaching the barrier with their tickets at the ready. Brandt felt his heart sink. He had seen that type in Germany often enough; they would shop their own mother.

The gendarme looked at Brandt, noted his wooden arm and the old crone with the saliva dribbling down her chin mumbling, *"Bon chance, mon fils,"* as she pressed Brandt's good hand, and dismissed him as harmless. Some stupid shit who had let his arm be shot off early in the war.

He looked at Gerda and recognised her for what she was — a Yid. He'd been in the Vichy *Milice* until he had seen which way the wind was blowing and had swiftly transferred back to the *Gendarmerie* in 1943. But during his time in that fascist police he had arrested Jews enough; he could recognise them with one eye closed.

"Papier" he demanded, delighted at the way she lost colour immediately, fear springing into her dark Jewess eyes.

She swallowed hard.

Brandt tensed. Next to the French cop the big American MP stopped chewing gum and stared at the girl who had suddenly gone an ashen white.

"Votre carte d'identité?" the French policeman rapped, knowing he had struck gold somehow. If she was Jewish why was she afraid? The Americans loved Jews, after all everyone knew their president, that cripple Roosevelt, was one. She should have nothing to fear.

Gerda looked at Brandt a little helplessly. He nodded encouragingly. "I'm afraid I forgot them. But I have my ticket."

Her French was perfect, the gendarme told himself, grammatically better than his own, but there was no mistaking that intonation. He had heard it often enough when working with Gestapo men who spoke French. She was a Jewess but she was a German one, too, and without papers.

"Stay there," he ordered briskly and, taking the big American by one arm, steered him out of earshot, not taking his hard suspicious gaze off the terrified girl for one moment.

Up on the platform their train was raising steam. People were closing doors and the guard had tugged his little horn out of his pocket and was preparing to blow it. It would be setting off in a moment. Brandt's brain raced electrically.

"She is not French," the cop said to the bored American in his laboured slow English.

"So what?" the big GI said rolling his gum from one side of his mouth to the other effortlessly.

"She might be a spy?"

"Jesus H!" the American said unimpressed, "you French see spies under the bed. What in Christ's name is there to spy on here?"

"She has no papers," the gendarme said haughtily, pulling himself up to his full height and glowering at the American who towered above him. "I have my duty."

"Well, do your frigging duty," the American suggested as Brandt flashed into action. He gave the old crone a shove. She shrieked and cannoned into the big American who gasped and went staggering back.

"Run for it, Gerda!" he yelled. "For God's sake run for the shitting train!"

"Sale con!" the gendarme yelled, recognising the German. He grabbed for his pistol.

Brandt didn't give him a chance. He swung his wooden arm. It connected with the gendarme's unshaven chin. He howled with pain and flew backwards, pistol falling out of suddenly nerveless fingers.

Somewhere a rifle cracked. A slug howled off the metal barrier close to Brandt. He turned round and fired in the same movement. A French soldier holding a rifle slumped to his knees.

Brandt wasted no more time. He grabbed Gerda by the hand. They raced forward. The guard tried to stop them holding out both hands wide, stretched as if they were escaping animals. Brandt didn't hesitate. Again he slammed his wooden fist into the man's face. The guard's nose split. He went down spitting out broken teeth, his face looking as if someone had just thrown a handful of strawberry jam at it.

Now a volume of ragged shots rang out. They ran for their lives. Bullets struck the concrete around their flying feet, striking up angry little blue sparks. They came parallel with the guard's van. An ugly bearded face peered out at them. *"Non ... non,"* the official yelled, *"c'est pas possible!"* He tried to close the door. *"C'est interdit —"* His words ended in a shriek as Brandt grabbed him brutally and swung him out and onto the platform. The next moment Brandt stamped his foot down on the official's face, hard.

"Quick ... *for God's sake get in!"* he cried and thrust Gerda into the empty guard's compartment as the Army NCOs came running down the platform, firing from the hip as they did so, their bullets striking the van, showering the two fugitives with splinters of wood.

Then it was too late. The train gathered speed. Great streams of thick black smoke swept backwards. The train turned the bend. The wild firing died away. Then they were gone, chugging up into the hills, and they had done it.

For a while they lay prostrate on the floor of the dirty van, their breath coming in short hectic gasps. Then slowly they roused themselves, knowing that they had little time to decide what to do next.

Brandt wiped his mouth with the back of his hand, wishing he had something strong to drink, watching the snowbound French countryside whiz by through the still open door of the van. He said, "They will surely telegraph ahead about us. Of course they'll have no communication with the driver of the locomotive. So unless they change the signals they'll have the cops waiting for us at the next stop for this train. We've got to be off before then. The question is where will that next stop be?"

She looked thoughtful. "I know this area a little. I should imagine we'll travel through the plain before going through the gap in the Vosges and then on to Dijon. If that's the case the next stop might well be Nancy."

"Nanzig," he said, using the old German name for the Lorraine capital. "How far is it from Verdun?"

"Sixty or seventy kilometres I suppose."

He referred to his watch, checking the telegraph poles as they passed, knowing that each one was exactly thirty metres from the other. After a minute he announced,

"I guess we're going at about fifty kilometres an hour. So that gives us about an hour to get out before we reach Nancy." He sucked his bottom lip thoughtfully and watched the barren countryside roll by. Even at fifty kilometres an hour it was too dangerous to jump out. Although they might not be killed at that speed they would certainly be injured and that would be the end for them. For Brandt had no illusions about what would happen if they were captured together. The French would be ruthless against the Germans, their former occupiers. They would shoot the both of them as spies in civilian clothing.

Gerda must have read his thoughts. "I know," she said simply, "it's dangerous, but we've got to do it."

He nodded. "But let's wait a while. There might be another gradient or something which will slow this thing down and then we go. Thank God for the snow. At least it'll break our fall."

So they relapsed into silence, each one of them wrapped in their own thoughts. But even as they did so they knew full well that time was running out fast. They had to do something, otherwise it would be too late.

TEN

"Verdammte Scheisse!" Skorzeny cursed. "Did you say that girl assistant of yours has vanished? Are you sure? Can she not be in the outer camp?"

At the other end of the line Professor von Gluck sweated uncomfortably. He ran his finger round the sweat-soaked rim of his collar as if it were suddenly too tight.

"Well?" Skorzeny demanded when there was no answer, holding the phone as if it were an offensive weapon.

"I am sure, Obersturmbannfuhrer. My people have looked. We even searched the latrines."

"The latrines?"

"Yes," the Professor explained uneasily. "Sometimes they murder each other by drowning the victim in the, er, shit, if you'll excuse the crudity, Obersturmbannfuhrer. Especially if they think their victim is too close to us Germans, as she was."

Skorzeny suddenly remembered the girl kneeling in front of the Professor with his flies underdone; but he didn't mention the fact that the missing girl had seemed very especially close to that fat pig of a scientist. "Only those Jewish sub-humans could think of anything so disgusting as that. Continue the search. That Jewess was no fool. She may well have guessed what the purpose of your experiments was. She must be found at all costs! Do you understand?"

"I shall do my utmost, Obersturmbannfuhrer. And there is something else."

"What?" Skorzeny rasped over the phone.

"I'm afraid to say that there has been a tragic loss. It was thought that you were still at Nordhausen so they called my office so that I could relay —"

"For God's sake, get on with it, man," Skorzeny snapped losing his patience.

"Herr Kapitanleutnant Brandt has been reported missing. Apparently he was flying —"

"I know where he was flying. Tell me the rest."

"It was a colonel from Luftwaffe air traffic control. He said that they had lost contact with Kapitanleutnant Brandt's plane west of Metz. He said so far they had no means of ascertaining what happened to it. They are listening to enemy frequencies and broadcasts to discover what the enemy might have to say on the matter ..." his voice trailed away to nothing for he sensed that at the other end in Berlin Skorzeny was not listening.

He wasn't. His mind was racing. What was he going to do he asked himself. Had Brandt been shot down and captured? If he had then the whole mission would be compromised. And where was the girl? He pulled himself together. "Herr Professor, keep up the search for the girl. I shall contact Luftwaffe HQ and see if they have any further news. *Auf Wiederhoren.*"

"Auf Wiederhoren," the Professor echoed the greeting but the phone at the other end had already gone dead. For a while the fat scientist sat there staring at the receiver. Slowly he put it down and considered his own position. He had sent the damned girl to Brandt's room.

The thought of her engaging in sex with a virile young officer, he told himself, might have some effect on his own flagging libido. He had imagined her in bed, totally naked, gasping with passion as he pushed his instrument into her brutally. Yes, he had felt a certain amount of delightful arousal at the thought.

Now she had disappeared altogether. She had not been seen since she went to Brandt's room. Had he taken her with him? It was a strong possibility. If he had and then somehow managed to get her on the plane to Lorient then both of them were either killed or in enemy hands.

He sucked his thick sensuous bottom lip and made his decision. He would wait till the evening. If she were not found by then he would report her dead, drowned in the latrine. He knew even the Gestapo would not have the latrines searched in an attempt to find her body. That would be the way out.

He forgot the Jewess and pressed the bell on his desk. There was big, strong-looking Russian wench working in the outer lab. He had noticed her several times. She had a full passionate mouth and strong, capable hands. He'd have her transferred to his section. She might be able to do it for him. Smiling, pleased with himself, feeling that he was handling the situation very well, he waited to give his orders for the woman to be brought to him.

Skorzeny was not pleased with himself and the way he was managing Operation New York. Already the operation might well be compromised and now he had apparently lost Doenitz's best U-boat skipper; and he knew there weren't many aces of Brandt's kind left at Doenitz's disposal. He told himself, after a few minutes, he'd worry about finding a replacement for the missing Brandt later.

He rose to his feet instead and stared at the big wall map of Greater New York City. Since the Fuhrer had first divulged the great secret to him, ten days ago now, a lot of detail had been added to the blank map which the Fuhrer had shown him. Now, as he ran his index finger over the map, he repeated the unfamiliar names to himself; the Hudson River; East River. He traced the five boroughs: Manhattan, Queens, the Bronx ... Brooklyn, Richmond, looking for the targets which his experts had decided would cause the most fear and alarm.

"The Statue of Liberty must go, of course," he told himself. That would be a primary target. It was the symbol of that decadent, plutocratic Yiddish city. There would have to be a target in the Queens, too, perhaps in the area of Forest Hill the tennis courts. The Queens was full of Jews. Yes, that definitely was a target. The two bridges and naturally the tunnel under the Hudson, that was obvious. Destroy the bridges and the tunnel and the city would grind to a stop. The place the Amis called Fifth Avenue, there, yes, that, too. That's where the plutocrats and Jewish bloodsuckers displayed their wealth in those vulgar stores and shops. His brow creased in a frown.

All these targets were excellent. He would have to congratulate his *Amerika-Experten* when it was all over. They had done a splendid job in selecting their targets. But as yet he had not seen one that would make the whole world rise to its feet when it was destroyed and cry, "New York is finished!" But what?

Outside it had begun to snow again. Soft sad little flakes were falling slowly in front of the window of this remote hunting lodge which was the HQ of Skorzeny's *Jagdkommando*. He turned from the map and watched the snow for a few moments. It reminded him just how fast time was running out. In December when the weather would be bad, snowy, foggy and the like, keeping the Allied airpower grounded, then the Fuhrer would attack. He had to be ready by then.

Suddenly, out of nowhere — later he could never explain how it happened — it came to him. He remembered the picture. He had returned from the student fencing school in Vienna proudly exhibiting his new sabre slash filled with black paste so that it would stay open and give him a permanent scar*, when one of the beery crowd of fellow students had cried, "Let's go to the cinema!"

[* In German and Austrian universities there were duelling societies among the various student fraternities. The aim was to achieve a couple of prominent facial scars which would mark a man out for what he was for the rest of his life.]

"No," others had answered, "let's get really filthy stinking drunk as usual."

But in the end they had crowded into the cinema annoying the other patrons with their loud calls and belches, breathing beer fumes over the protestors when they had been stopped dead by what they saw on the screen. He could remember the grainy flickering old film to this day. There, hanging to the side of a typical American skyscraper there was a huge ape, clutching a tiny, half-naked blonde in its ugly paw. Afterwards, when they had overcome their shock at the scene, he had whispered to his neighbour, "Klaus, could a chimp really be as big as that?"

"Of course not, Otto, you silly idiot. That was the Empire State Building, the tallest building in the world. It was all an optical illusion or something."

"The tallest building in the world," he remembered the words exactly although it was over a decade since he had first heard them in that broken down Viennese fleapit where the ushers came round periodically to spray the air with perfume to hide the smell.

"Of course," he said out loud, "that's it. What better object to symbolise to the world that New York is finished." He stopped short his sallow face flushed with excitement as someone knocked softly on the map room door. Hastily he slid the curtain back in front of the top secret map and said, *"Herein."*

It was Hartung his signals officer. "We've just received an enigma, sir. From Leutnant Schulze at Lorient."

Skorzeny tried to forget the new key target for a moment. He snapped, "Read it, please, Hartung."

Hartung cleared his throat as if he were about to address a public meeting and Skorzeny told himself the middle-aged signals officer was not really the type the *Jagdkommando* needed. He was too pompous. Still he was a good signals officer.

"Beg to report. Group Schulze is ready for operations. Beg to inform you further that U-boats 1221, 1222, 1223, 1224, 1225 and 1226 are said to have been completed. Beg to suggest that 1221 with Group Schulze on board should be given permission to sail almost immediately. Would make it easier for landing if left before November storms habitual on that coast. End. Schulze."

Skorzeny shook his head in mock wonder. "I hope that fellow Schulze's American is better than his German? All that 'beg' to this and 'beg' that. No matter." He fell silent for a few moments while Hartung waited attentively. Skorzeny knew that it would take a while longer before Professor von Gluck's special V-2 would be ready for transportation by E-boat to Lorient. He knew, too, that the longer Group Schulze remained in place the more risk they ran of being apprehended by the enemy authorities. But they had to be landed safely. Without them the great plan might fail, just as the current haphazard V-2 bombardment of London was not having the success the Fuhrer had intended and expected because there were no means of knowing where the missiles had landed.

"All right," he broke his silence finally, "Send this."

"Sir?"

"Authorise you to start off Group Schulze within next forty-eight hours. Report successful landing to U —" he clicked his fingers.

"U-1221," Hartung helped him.

"Yes, thank you, to U-1221 within twenty four hours of landing. Oh, yes. *Hals and Beinbruch**. Skorzeny." Hartung waited and Skorzeny said, "That's it. Get it into the Enigma at once. And bring me the acknowledgement of receipt from Lorient as soon as you have it, Hartung."

"Zu Befehl, Obersturmbannfuhrer," Hartung clicked his heels and went leaving Skorzeny staring at the softly falling snow, his mind full of pictures of a burning Empire State Building falling to the ground, below tiny screaming figures, all with large Jewish noses, scuttling for safety.

"We've got it, sir," Fleming burst into the Admiral's office without knocking, "we've got it!"

Outside an elderly rating cleaning the corridor was singing softly and tunelessly, *"Hitler's only one ball/Goering's is very small Himmler's is somewhat sim'lar! But Doctor Goebbels's no balls at all ..."*

"We've got what?" the Admiral demanded a little annoyed as he looked up from the Jane strip in the *Daily Mirror.* This week the forces' heroine was down to her frilly knickers again in the cause of Allied victory and he liked to take time with his study of her delightful figure.

"Straight from Bletchley, sir, an Ultra." He waved the top secret decode in front of him as if it were a flag of victory.

The Admiral sighed. These "wavy navy" types like Fleming would never learn how to conduct themselves as real naval officers. "All right, Ian, let me have it."

"Yes sir. Bletchley's just decoded a message sent by SS Major Skorzeny. You know, the chap with the ugly mug who kidnapped Mussolini last year from the Gran Sasso and whisked him off to Vienna."

* Literally, break your neck and legs, i.e. happy landings.

The Admiral nodded, face suddenly tense. This time Fleming really seemed to have something.

"Well, sir, Skorzeny has authorised a *'Gruppe Schulze'* to sail, presumably by sub, within the next forty-eight hours."

"So?" the Admiral appeared confused.

"Well, Schulze is the *Leutnant* with whom my nancy boy is having an affair. That's the one who boasted he was going to be involved in a *ganz grosse Sache."*

"Dammit, Ian, I wish you wouldn't use all that damned Boche talk! They've been a bloody nuisance as it is for the last five years, so I certainly don't want to hear their damned ugly language as well."

"Sorry, sir. Well, he was the officer who was to take part, in his words, in a 'very big thing'. Now he appears to be in charge of a group of men who presumably, like him, are fluent English speakers, which means they are intended for some kind of sabotage or spying mission."

The Admiral nodded his understanding. "All right, Ian," he said after some consideration. "I think we need Commander Savage in on this one. If anyone can see these Boche chaps off in their U —"

"U-1221." Just like Hartung, Fleming supplied the U-boat's number hurriedly.

"Thank you. Well, as I was saying, old Killer Savage is our man."

ELEVEN

For about ten minutes now the French train had been running along the River Mosélle and Brandt had noticed that whenever the train came to one of the many bridges across the winding river it slowed down considerably. He assumed that during the five years of war little had been done to ensure that the bridges were maintained so that now, as a safety measure, the driver slowed down.

His mind made up he turned to Gerda who was shivering again in the freezing cold of the guard's van and said, "The next bridge."

"What?"

"We go at the next bridge. Over the side and into the water. I know it'll be freezing but the water should break our fall. Somewhere or other we'll get dry. But first things first. All right? You're not afraid?"

"Yes, but not with you." She looked at him with those dark eyes of hers, full of devotion and love.

His heart went out to her. He pressed her cold hand gently. "Don't you worry. Everything will be all right. We'll get out of this mess and then —" He stopped short. The train was beginning to slow down. "Get ready," he snapped urgently. "It looks as if we're coming to another bridge across the Mosélle." She rose to her feet. "You're going first. Don't be afraid. Just close your eyes and jump when I tell you to."

The train was now going about fifteen kilometres an hour as it edged round the bend towards the simple steel bridge which looked to Brandt as if it had been recently re-erected; perhaps the original had been destroyed in the recent fighting in this area. He looked down at the river. It was about ten metres below the bridge. Not bad, he told himself, and prayed the water below was not too shallow, deep enough to break their fall.

"Get near the door now," he commanded, sounding more confident than he felt. He took her by the elbow and guided her to the door of the van. Although the train was slowing down it still seemed to him to be going damned fast. But this was their last chance. He had to take the risk. They were almost in the centre of the bridge now. He could hear the hollow clatter of the wheels going over the sleepers. He took a deep breath and yelled, *"Now!"*

She jumped, her eyes pressed tightly together. He saw her strike the water. Then he jumped too.

He gasped with shock as he struck the water. The Mosélle was freezing. He went under and came up gasping and spluttering, spitting out the icy water he had swallowed. He flashed a look upwards. Already the train was disappearing around the next bend. No one had seen them it appeared.

"Gerda," he called thickly.

"Over here, quick!" She was swimming to the far bank. He followed her as best he could with his one hand, cursing again the wooden arm which always made him feel off-balance in water. Moments later they were crouched together among the skeletal trees on the far bank, teeth chattering, faces blue with cold, but triumphant that they had escaped the train without being discovered.

"All right," Brandt said when he had recovered his breath. "Those mountains up there," he indicated the snow-capped peaks to the west, they're the Vosges Mountains. If I remember my geography correctly we've got to work to the south of them. There's a pass there, I've forgotten its name now, but I know there is one."

She rose to her feet, soaked and shivering. "I'm ready," she said simply.

"Brave girl. Come on then. As the stubble-hoppers say; it's march or croak from here onwards."

Gerda forced a smile. "March or croak," she echoed. "I think I prefer the former."

"Then we march."

They did. For a while they stuck to the fields. But the snow was too deep and the going hard and after a while they took to the country roads which were not too bad as carts and vehicles had been down them and flattened the snow. Now they moved fast. They both knew they had to if they didn't want to land in trouble on account of their soaked clothing. Their breath ringed their faces in a grey cloud as they panted, they walked swiftly, saying little, swinging their arms in an exaggerated fashion to keep the circulation moving. But as they walked Brandt knew they'd have to find shelter and warmth soon. To the east the sky was turning a leaden grey which indicated more snow and an icy wind was blowing across the fields. He told himself that they were now in Alsace and that the peasants here were all German-speaking. Indeed, the Fuhrer had made them Germans once again back in '40, booty Germans, as they had been laughed at behind their backs. Many of their menfolk were still fighting with the German Wehrmacht. Perhaps they would help? He hoped so.

By two it was snowing hard once more. The wind whipped the icy flakes mercilessly into their strained blue faces and every fresh step was a torture. Brandt could see that Gerda was failing. She kept lagging behind. But she didn't protest when he urged her to keep up. Instead she said, "Sorry ... I'm a burden on you."

To which he replied, "Of course you're not, Gerda. You're doing splendidly. Now then, remember, march or croak."

"March or croak."

By three, with the snow showing no mercy and falling in a solid white stream as if it would never stop again, Brandt knew they couldn't go on much longer. They had to find shelter and warmth. Up to now they had skirted the little hamlets and villages which were everywhere on the plain: usually collections of white-painted half-timbered medieval houses clustered around the customary onion-towered church.

Now he determined they would seek help in the next one they encountered. But from whom? He decided it would be no use approaching the wealthier farmers and wine-growers found at the edges of these Alsatian villages. They had most to lose and wouldn't be prepared to take risks. That left the ordinary peasants, perhaps the local priest, so that meant they would have to go to the centre of the village where those people lived. It would be risky, he knew that. They might be spotted by a local policeman or the mayor, both of whom would be loyal to the French government he assumed. But that was a chance they would have to take.

Twenty minutes later they blundered, blinded by snow, right into a village almost before they knew where they were, the snow was that thick.

Gerda looked at him a little shocked, but she hadn't the strength left to question. Numbly she nodded her head in agreement when he said, "We've got to find shelter ... can't go like this much longer, Gerda ... It's getting dark, too. Come on."

Blinded by the whirling snow they stumbled on. Already the little Alsatian village was locked up for the night. Everywhere the wooden shutters had been closed and there was no sign of the animals usual to such places. There was not even a single dog. But the place was inhabited all right. They could smell the sweet smell of wood smoke coming from the chimneys and now and again they caught a snatch of muted talk from behind the shutters. Once they heard someone scraping away mercilessly at a violin.

The church loomed up. It was the usual domed structure with the usual statue outside of a Marieanne supporting a heroically dying *poilu* and carrying the tricolour. "We'll try there," Brandt gasped, supporting Gerda who was virtually out on her feet. "That house next door where the light's coming from will be where the priest lives."

She nodded numbly unable to speak.

Brandt staggered to the door and, taking the long metal bell-pull in his frozen hand, tugged hard. Somewhere deep inside the house there was a muted pealing. For a long moment nothing happened. Then there was the hollow sound of heavy boots coming slowly along a stone-flagged corridor, as if their owner was considering whether he should go to the door or not. A rusty squeak, the turn of a lock and the big oak door swung open.

A large man dressed in a cassock stood there gazing at them as they blinked their eyes in the sudden light. His face was neither friendly nor unfriendly, simply neutral. *"Vous desirez?"* he asked in French and when he saw that Brandt didn't react followed in Alsatian German. *"Was wollen Sie?"*

Brandt was too far gone to lie. They needed warmth and shelter fast. "I'm an escaped German prisoner," he said. "The girl has helped me. We want food and shelter, Herr Pfarrer. Will you help?"

"Yes, of course. Straightaway." The priest's voice was suddenly strong and decisive. "Come on in." He turned and stood to one side so that they could stagger in, tears springing to their eyes as the warmth hit them after the freezing cold outside.

Hurriedly he closed the door behind him and rang the little bell which rested on the hall table. "My housekeeper will bring you something hot immediately. Now, follow me into the salon. It is good and warm."

"Thank you, thank you," the two of them gasped hardly daring to believe their own luck. They had been saved again.

Half an hour later they had been fed an enormous dish of sauerkraut and sausage, washed down with scalding hot coffee laced with brandy, eaten under the beaming gaze of a very fat housekeeper dressed in what Brandt took to be the traditional Alsatian costume. The priest, for his part, seemed detached and distant, coming in from time to time, puffing at his pipe but saying nothing. Though Brandt noted his dark eyes were restless like those of a man who had problems.

They sat in front of the roaring tiled stove listening carefully as the priest explained the position to them, hearing for the first time, now the storm had died away, the rumble of the guns in the distance. "We are about thirty kilometres from the front here, Herr Kapitanleutnant," he said. "The Americans are fighting in Lorraine and in the Saar. Their troops are everywhere in the rearline villages, waiting to go up and coming down for rest. So far we have not had them here for which I am thankful. The Americans have a bad reputation with our women-folk. There have been numerous cases of rape," he lowered his voice as if the word itself was dirty but kept his eyes on Gerda's face. , "So the rear areas are full of their counter-intelligence agents. The Americans have a phobia about German spies so I shall be able to keep you only for the night. It is too dangerous. But I will give you the address of another priest, a great friend from my seminary days who will put you up on the other side of the Vosges."

"I understand. Thank you," Brandt said slowly savouring another hot drink of coffee laced with brandy. "We shall be glad of one night out of the cold."

"I suggest that when you have finished your drink you turn in for the night. People around here go to bed with the chickens," the priest chuckled but there was no answering warmth in his eyes which, for some reason, he couldn't keep off Gerda. "The villagers might get a little suspicious if the priest kept his lights burning longer than usual."

"Yes, I see," Brandt said and drained the rest of his coffee. He looked at Gerda. She nodded and did the same. They were exhausted anyway.

A few minutes later they were mounting the creaking stairs to the bedroom, following the housekeeper who was hugging two hot bricks, wrapped in a towel to her ample bosom. They would be placed in the bottom of their bed she had explained. "They'll keep you warm, afterwards," she said and winked knowingly so that Gerda blushed and Brandt asked himself what exactly the relationship was between the priest and the fat housekeeper.

But there was no "afterwards". Almost immediately their heads touched the stiff white pillows, smelling of camphor, they fell into a deep sleep.

Gerda awoke with a start. The blackout was down and she could see through the window. There was a spectral moon and the dark velvet of the sky was studded with hard silver stars. For a moment she wondered where she was. Then she remembered and could hear the soft breathing of Brandt next to her in the snug bed. She gave a little sigh of contentment and prepared to snuggle down next to him once more when she heard the sound, similar to the one which must have woken her.

Now she was completely awake. Something or somebody was walking as softly as possibly over the hard frozen surface of the snow. She pulled up Brandt's hand and looked at the green glowing dial of his wristwatch. It was two in the morning. Who would be about at this time of the day in such weather?

She didn't hesitate. Careful not to wake him, shivering as her bare feet touched the cold wooden floor, she moved to the window and, careful not to show herself, peered down below.

A man stood in the shadows cast by the snow-heavy trees, watching the house. She stared hard but could make out nothing. Were her eyes playing tricks on her? No, another man appeared out of the silver gloom. This one had a rifle slung over his shoulder and on his head he wore the boxlike *képi* of the *Gendarmerie.* They were cops!

She gasped with shock. There could be only one reason why there were armed policemen outside the house at this time of night. The priest or his housekeeper had betrayed them.

TWELVE

Carefully, very carefully, Brandt came down the narrow stairs, pistol in hand. Behind him, hardly daring to breathe, Gerda followed. Down below they could hear soft voices talking in a whisper. They were talking in French and Brandt guessed they were police from the nearest big town.

Despite the coldness of the stairs Brandt felt himself sweating. He knew that the faintest noise would give them away and he didn't stand much of a chance against the half-dozen armed police they had already counted outside in the shadows. As he had whispered to Gerda only moments before, "Our only chance is to steal their car. They must have come by one and stationed it somewhere on the outskirts of the village so that we wouldn't hear it driving up."

They reached the bottom step. The door of the study to their left was slightly open and he could hear the mutter of voices coming from behind it. Gerda strained her ears and then whispered into Brandt's ear. "The priest is telling them that you're a German and I'm a Jewess. He recognised that at once."

Brandt shook his head in sadness. There seemed no hope for Jews like Gerda. Everybody, even priests of the Catholic church seemed to hate them.

"Damn them!" he whispered back. "Come on." On tiptoe, taking exaggerated strides, they headed for the door. Brandt said a silent prayer that it wouldn't squeak when he opened it. It didn't. A fierce, icy wind buffeted their faces. Brandt didn't mind. It would drown any noise they might make. He crouched, pistol at the ready and surveyed his immediate front. He already knew where the cops were to the rear of the house. Were there any to the front?

He caught the soft glimmer of a cigarette end. A cop was having a quick smoke in the shelter of the church. Good, he told himself, that was that one out of the way. But were there anymore? He looked again then said, "I think it's all clear. Let's go."

They moved from the shelter of the house and Brandt cursed at the noise their feet made crunching over the frozen snow. He prayed that the howl of the wind would cover it.

They turned into the village street. All was silent. Nothing stirred. With Gerda at his side they worked their way forward through the shadows cast by the little half-timbered houses. Now the only sound was that of the wind and their own harsh breathing. Once Brandt stopped and cocked his head to one side. He thought he had heard a sound from the direction of the priest's house but he had been mistaken. Still it wouldn't be long before the cops found that they had gone. Then all hell would be let loose.

He quickened his pace automatically and whispered out of the side of his mouth, "We should see the car soon. Cops don't usually like to walk far, the fat bastards. As soon as —" He stopped short. From behind what looked like a large barn to his left there came the steady throb of an engine.

"That's it," he whispered urgently. "Running the engine to keep warm out of this damned wind." He thought hard. "You stay here, Gerda."

"But —"

"No buts. I don't want you getting hurt. I'll fare better when I'm not worrying about you." She nodded her understanding. "All right. Here I go. I'll whistle three times when I get the car. You come running then. *Fast!*"

"Be careful."

"I will. Don't worry." Then he was gone, slipping into the shadows, half crouched, automatic at the ready.

A minute later he saw the car. It was a long black Citroen that seemed bent in the middle. He flashed a look to left and right. Nobody. He crept forward. He wouldn't use the gun unless he was forced to. Now he could see the driver's outline behind the fogged-up windows, the green dashboard line colouring his face a sickly hue. He appeared to be asleep. At least his eyes were closed. Brandt prayed that he was. It would make the job easier.

He approached the door, the steady throb of the motor drowning the sound his boots made on the frozen snow. He thrust his pistol into his belt. With his right hand he grasped the door handle hardly daring to breathe. Inside the man didn't stir. Now Brandt could see him quite clearly. His *képi* was tilted to the back of his shaven head and he was leaning back, chest rising and falling faintly.

Brandt licked suddenly parched lips. His heart was racing. At his temples a vein ticked violently. It was now or never. Soon they'd discover the birds had flown at the priest's house.

"One ... two ... three," Brandt counted off the seconds to himself. *"Now!"* he flung the door open suddenly.

"Que —" the driver cried, eyes opening. Not for long. Brandt's wooden fist crashed into his startled face. He yelled with pain, blood spurting from a broken nose. Brandt grabbed him. The man fell to the snow moaning and staining it with his blood. He opened his mouth perhaps to shout for help. Brandt didn't give him a chance. His boot lashed out. The driver's head flopped to one side and Brandt heard something snap like a brittle branch underfoot in a dry summer. He was either unconscious or dead, Brandt didn't care which. He hadn't time.

He flashed a look inside. Empty. He flung himself behind the driver's seat and, winding down the window, whistled shrilly three times in the same instant that he thrust home first gear.

Gerda came running as he gunned the motor impatiently, already flinging open the passenger door for her to enter.

Suddenly, startlingly, things began to go wrong. The door of the barn was flung open. A cop stood there outlined in the yellow light. He took in the situation at once. He raised his carbine and fired in one and the same movement. A slug howled off the bonnet.

A whistle shrilled the alarm. Someone shouted an angry order. Boots came pelting over the snow. "Run, Gerda ... run," he cried desperately as one of the running cops tried to head her off. He drew his pistol and fired. Scarlet flame stabbed the silver gloom. The cop flung up his hands as if he were climbing an invisible ladder and then flopped to the snow on his knees, head bent, moaning.

Another took up the chase. Brandt fired again and missed. He pushed the pistol back into his belt. Hurriedly he thrust home reverse, grinding the gears with tension. He let out the clutch. The Citroen shot backwards. A bullet shattered the rear window. For a moment he was blinded *"Scheisse!"* he cursed in frustration. He swung the car round in first and fumbled to turn on the lights. Suddenly they were blazing. He saw her running all out. Ten metres behind her was one of the cops. There were others everywhere a little further off. He caught a glimpse of the treacherous priest and the fat housekeeper waving their hands and cheering as if this was some kind of game.

He started forward. Shots were howling off the chassis everywhere. He knew his luck wouldn't last much longer. Somebody would hit a tyre and that would be it.

Now she was only metres away. He could see every strained feature of her ashen face as she pelted towards the car, head thrown back, hair streaming in the wind, eyes full of terror. "I'm coming!" he cried above the snap-and-crack of the firing and the roar of his engine, "Hold on Ger —"

The cry died on his lips. She had stumbled and gone down on one knee. "Get up!" he roared fervently.

"I can't," she cried back, tears of despair starting to stream down her poor face. "I'm finished."

A burst of sub-machinegun fire ripped the length of the Citroen. He felt the slugs tug and tweak at his jacket. But the seat saved him from any serious wound. A man ran round the corner. He levelled the sub-machinegun again.

"Go," she screamed. "They won't harm me. *Go!*" The cop aimed. Brandt made the most awesome decision he had ever made, knowing she was right. They couldn't do anything to her but they would shoot him.

He swung the car round in the same instant that the cop fired from the hip. Slugs struck the ground all about where he had been. Vicious blue sparks and chips of stone erupted on the wall of the house opposite. Next minute he was careening around the bend in the road out of the village and heading for the open country, the sound of the firing already dying away behind him, feeling sick at heart and more wretched than he had ever been in all his young life.

"Now, first we are going to have some fun," the Gendarme sergeant said unbuttoning his flies while the others gawped and smirked. Five minutes before they had sent the priest and his housekeeper to their beds, telling the traitors, "You have done well. Be assured that the Prefect will hear of your great service to France." Now, while they waited for another car to come from Belfort and pick them up they said to her, "Might as well enjoy yourself before they put you against the wall and shoot you."

Instinctively she knew from their leers and hoarse grunts of approval what they were going to do to her. She shrank against the wall, arms outspread, face contorted with terror like a trapped animal which knows there is no escape.

The sergeant pulled out his organ and showed it to the others proudly. It was already erect. He advanced on her his penis swinging like a club. She stared at it horrified. He laughed. "Get a good look. You'll be feeling it in half a moment — and others as well."

He flung out one hand. He caught her dress and ripped it straight down the centre. She could feel his breath on her now. It stank of cheap tobacco and garlic. With both hands he reached for her waist. She tried to resist but he was too strong for her. He grunted and with one hand ripped down her knickers to her knees. With the other he directed his penis into her, pinning her against the wall. Savagely he thrust it home. She screamed, "No, no," she pleaded, "please not!"

Her appeal seemed to rouse him to greater efforts. Panting hard, as if he were running a great race, he thrust himself into her time and time again brutally. Suddenly his body contorted. A spasm of what seemed pain contorted his cruel face. "Shit!" he cursed and then fell from her weakly, all passion spent, his organ flaccid. "Who's next?" he asked in a weak voice as she slumped sobbing as if her heart were broken.

An hour later they flung her into a stinking freezing cell in Belfort. "The judge will deal with you tomorrow, bitch," the Gendarme sergeant said. "I don't doubt that it will be all over soon." He leered down at her as she slumped down on the floor, still crying. "But if you're lucky I'll come and see you again beforehand." He laughed cruelly and touched the bulge in his breeches. "You know what I've got in here, don't you now, and you like it, bitch. I could feel it. Maybe I'll give you one last taste of it before they chop off yer turnip. *Adieu.*"

How long she lay there weeping she didn't know. She was too concerned with the pain, the humiliation, the horror of that rape. It had gone on forever it seemed: a procession of grunting, swearing, panting men, who bit her breasts, tugged at her buttocks cruelly and thrust themselves into her until her whole body seemed aflame with pain.

But as the light started to filter reluctantly through the dirty barred window, she looked around her through eyes which were swollen and red with sobbing. She saw a cement bunk chained to the wall, a rickety table which would collapse if she stood upon it to hang herself and the piss bucket in the corner, scarred enamel and evil smelling.

She stared at the bucket dully. She knew she couldn't stand any more. The world and its cruelty were too much for her. Outside there was the jingle of keys. A flap in the door was opened. She caught a glimpse of a shaven head, then a mug and a pannikin of what looked like soup plus a hunk of bread were placed on the floor.

Breakfast she told herself. But she didn't reach out for the food or drink. She wanted neither. All she wanted was to die. But how? Again she continued to stare stupidly at the enamel piss-bucket. Time passed leadenly. On the floor the food went cold and congealed. Outside there was the sound of marching feet crunching over the hard-pressed snow. She didn't seem to hear.

Slowly, very slowly, she started to crawl over to the bucket, her body throbbing with pain, blood trickling down the inside of her thighs. She reached it and lay by it almost exhausted, waiting for the mist which threatened to overcome her to clear. The window, the bed, the bucket swung back into focus. She took a deep breath and forced herself to peer inside the filthy, lime-encrusted pail. Inside the enamel was jagged and broken everywhere to reveal the metal beneath. It was what she had anticipated. She reached and tugged at a sliver of the enamel. It was razor-sharp and cut her fingers, but that didn't matter now. She tugged again. The piece came away. She raised it and stared at the enamel almost stupidly. Slowly she drew it across her right wrist. The blood welled up almost immediately, thick, red, life-giving blood. Suddenly she gave a chuckle of mad, slobbering delight at her own cunning. She would escape them yet.

THIRTEEN

"Lorient," Brandt said to himself as he breasted the hill and saw the port spread out below him with the Atlantic beyond glittering a bright green in the winter sunshine.

It was two days now since he had abandoned the battered police car as soon as it had run out of gas; he knew he didn't have a chance in hell of getting any more. Since then he had marched along back roads, hitching lifts with peasants and once with the driver of a three-ton truck who he suspected was doing some black market deal or other off the main route.

Now he was very tired, dirty, unshaven so that he might well have been taken for some down-at-heel tramp at the end of his tether. Indeed, he didn't bother to detour round the villages any more. Instead he trudged through them, stopping to buy a hunk of black market bread and some cheese if he was lucky and passing on to wolf down the food in some convenient hiding place.

He squatted with his back to a tree, enjoying the faint warmth of the sun on his face after the snows of eastern France and stared at the port. The Americans, he knew, had called off their attempt to capture the port the month before after the high losses they had suffered capturing other French ports such as St Lô and Brest. Instead they had surrounded the place with a green infantry division and driven on eastwards, right to the border of the Reich. Now Lorient was a besieged garrison supplied by air and sea from the Reich.

From his vantage point he could see the Ami positions quite clearly. It was obvious they had taken over most of the surrounding hamlets and farmhouses, their vehicles were everywhere. Here and there he could make out their gun batteries with tiny figures going about their business around the camouflaged cannon. But there was no continuous line. He could see gaps in the US positions of up to what he judged to be several hundred metres. Naturally the Amis would have patrols linking up their positions, especially at night, but he thought with a bit of luck he might slip through without being detected.

But where exactly? He studied the scene below carefully, debating with himself as he did so whether he would make his attempt during daylight hours or after dark. To the extreme right of the American line, almost on the cliff top, there was a patch of forest which did reach the edge of the sea itself. He knew Lorient of old. Once he had been stationed there for nearly a year and he knew that at certain tides small beaches appeared out of the sea at the bottom of those cliffs. With a bit of luck he could find one that would get him into Lorient without being observed from above. Then would come the problem of the German defenders. Undoubtedly they would have mines sown everywhere in the shallows; they would be taking no chances of the Amis attempting a sneak surprise attack. But he would worry about that problem when he got to it. The first thing was to make his way through the enemy lines.

In the end he decided to make the attempt in daylight. He didn't fancy his chances of going down the cliff with one hand under the cover of darkness, so he set off listening to the sound of the guns and chatter of machineguns to the far left of the besieged port. Some sort of sally or local attack was going on which made him glad. It would keep the enemy occupied. Now, as he approached the American positions, he could see that there were still farmers working in the fields, strewing the contents of their privies on the ploughed soil in preparation for next year's crops. He nodded his approval. If there were other civilians about he wouldn't stick out in particular.

An hour later he was approaching the enemy on the extreme right flank. American infantrymen were moving about casually, hands in pockets, rifles slung carelessly over their shoulders. Another group was lining up in the shelter of a wall while one of their members placed a tin bowl around the head of a seated soldier and started to snip away at his hair with hand clippers. From a barn there came the clatter of tin pans and the rich smell of cooking food and coffee, something which made his stomach rumble with hunger. But no one seemed to take the slightest notice of him. For them he was just another broken down "Frog".

He raised a weary smile at the thought. What would they have said if they had known he was a German U-boat commander whose task it was to bring terror and sudden death to one of their greatest cities on the other side of the Atlantic?

He left the American outpost behind. He passed a tumbled own cottage. Someone had been digging the garden and had left it half finished with a fork still stuck in the rich soil. Brandt didn't hesitate. He grabbed the fork and thrust it over his shoulder. Now he felt much easier. He was a French peasant going about the mysterious businesses of French peasants everywhere.

He plodded down the dirt road. To left and right there were two machinegun posts, Both manned by helmeted infantry and Brandt guessed the soldiers were guarding the approaches from the sea. Even at this distance Brandt could tell they were bored by the task. For they stood around in groups smoking and chatting, not watching the sea as they should have been doing.

Brandt knew he would have to go through them before he disappeared into the trees. It was no use trying to cross into the fields where he was. They would notice. No, he had to keep on. Heart beating with tension he did so, head bent a little as if he were weary with his labours.

He came parallel with them. He could smell the rich odour of American tobacco. Perhaps he should stop and pretend to beg a cigarette from them as he had seen French civilians do during his journey here. But he decided against it; they might ask for papers or identification. He passed the first machinegun post. The GIs didn't appear to notice him. They kept on chatting, laughing occasionally in the bored way of men who knew each other too well with nothing new to tell.

He tramped by another couple of soldiers who were throwing some kind of hard ball at each other. He could hear the ball slam into their palms. Now he was almost level with the second machinegun post. A big man with red hair and a lot of inverted stripes on his sleeve was bellowing something into a walkie-talkie while another couple of NCOs listened in a casual sort of way.

Brandt shifted his shovel from one shoulder to the other as if he had been carrying it for a long time. The gesture, he thought, also hid his face which he believed didn't look too French. Now he was almost past the American post. Still his nerves tingled electrically. One slip now and he was sunk.

"Hey, Joe." It was the red-haired sergeant with the walkie-talkie he had just passed. "What's that Frog doing passing our lines?"

Joe, standing by the machinegun, looked up from the comic book he was reading and said in broken French, *"Pierre ... ou papier,* eh?"

Brandt felt a cold finger of fear trace its way down his spine. He had understood enough of the two languages to know they were stopping him for his identification papers. He forced himself to continue walking slowly, his eyes searching his front frantically. The nearest trees were still fifty metres away and behind him there were at least a dozen armed men.

"Stop," Joe commanded and, tossing aside his comic book, clambered out of his weapon pit.

Brandt stopped. There was no mistaking the harsh click of a safety catch being slipped off a rifle. With his good hand he gripped the shaft of his stolen shovel more firmly listening to Joe coming up the trail to check his non-existent papers.

"Kay, Buddy, let's see 'em," Joe said easily. It was clear from his tone that he thought he was totally in charge of the situation. *"Tournez ... papier ... vite —"* the rest of his demand ended in a howl of pain as in one and the same movement Brandt swung round and lashed out with the flat blade of the shovel.

Joe hurtled backwards holding his face, blood arching out of his shattered nose in a scarlet stream. "What —" he gasped as everywhere the others watched dumbfounded, caught completely by surprise by the French civilian's violent reaction.

Brandt didn't give them time to recover. He flung the shovel to the earth. Then he was running as he had never run before, zigzagging wildly across the ploughed field, heading for the cover of the trees. Suddenly the Americans started to react. Shots rang out.

Slugs kicked up the earth in little spurts all around his flying feet. But luck was on his side. A moment later he was blundering into the trees, the branches lashing at his face as he ran through them, going all out, praying that no root would trip him up: for already he could hear them yelling orders and men were beginning to run after him. He pressed on.

Now he could hear the roar of the sea and smell the clean salt air. He wasn't far from the edge of the cliff. He kept on going. Behind him the firing had ceased now but he could still hear their shouts; they were entering the wood, spreading out in a line, he guessed, assuming that he would be trapped once he got to the edge of the cliff.

Panting hard, lathered in sweat, he started to plough his way through a tangle of bramble bushes, telling himself the bushes would stop the Americans, too. It might well give him a few minutes in his attempt to get down the cliff ahead. He broke free.

There was the cliff edge. He stumbled and staggered towards it. He could hear them quite clearly in the trees now. He paused at the edge, chest heaving frantically, and stared down at the white wash of the sea beating at the land. He couldn't see if there was a beach down there, however small, because half way down the cliff bulged out and hid the shore. But he could see there was a rough path leading downwards. He'd have to take his chance. If he could get down below the bulge in the cliff before they reached the edge he'd be safe from their bullets at least.

Hesitating no longer, slipping and sliding more than once, fearing that he would go right over, Brandt began the descent, praying that he would reach the bulge in time. Seagulls soared back and forth all around in alarm, crying out like lost children. Once he caught his foot in a pothole and nearly went right over. He caught himself just in time.

"Over here," he heard someone cry close by. "He's over here, sarge!"

"Shit!" Brandt gasped and renewed his efforts, sliding down the tremendously steep track in a shower of chalk and pebbles. Firing broke out once more. Again slugs ripped the ground all around him. Once he yelped with pain and thought he had been hit by a bullet. But it was only a pebble. A slug slammed into his wooden arm and the impact nearly flung him off the cliff. He gasped with shock but caught himself. He went on. Now the bulge was looming up and he wondered how he was going to get over it without plunging onto the sea-tossed rocks below.

Up above they had set up a light machinegun of some sort. He could hear the *B-r-r-r* as they sprayed the cliff face with slugs. He knew his luck would not hold out much longer. No one bore that kind of charmed life. Now he edged his way to the left of the bulge, chalk erupting and flying everywhere. He had moments left. He knew that.

He peered over the bulge. There was a beach there after all. It was a tiny one of shining wet sand, perhaps only two or three metres broad, trapped in a little inlet behind the rocks and some ten metres below the bulge. Dare he, he asked himself. If he broke a leg down there he was finished; and if he missed and landed on the rocks he was a dead man.

Another vicious burst of machine-gun fire only a metre away made his mind up for him. Praying like he had never prayed before, Brandt launched himself into space, hurtling down to the sea and rocks below. At a tremendous rate the little beach raced up to meet him. He felt his breath ripped from his lungs. His ears were full of a loud roaring. Now his world was filled with the white angry tossing roaring waves, the great cruel boulders and that narrow stretch of wet brown sand. Would he make it?

Next moment he hit the sand with a great blow which sent a shock wave coursing violently through his body. His wooden arm snapped. Something hit him a gigantic blow in the stomach. He vomited. Next moment everything went black.

It was thus that the little naval patrol, four sailors and a middle-aged petty officer, found him sprawled face downwards and half buried with sand, smeared with his blood, the broken-off wooden hand a metre or so away from the prostrate body.

"Holy strawsack!" the petty officer cried in surprised shock as they trudged round the corner, weapons at the ready, "Cast yer frigging glassy orbs on that!"

"Done himself in then, has he, the poor shit," one of the sailors asked slowly, for inside Lorient they were all on starvation rations and were unable to act or speak swiftly.

"Suppose so," the petty officer agreed. "Gives us something to report when we get back." He grunted and pushed the toe of his boot underneath the still body. Another grunt and he turned it over on its back.

The Frenchman's face was a nasty sight, bruised and bleeding everywhere with a deep cut from one side of the forehead to the other. "I think ... I think he's breathing," the petty officer began slowly and then, with a gasp of surprise, "This is Kapitanleutnant Brandt!" he exclaimed.

"You mean the U-boat ace?" one of the patrol said. "What in shit is he doing here?" another asked unconvinced.

"Stop asking stupid questions," the petty officer snapped with some of his old strength. "Come on, let's drag him higher up the beach. Then you, Schmitt, had better get back to HQ and report this, tootsweet!"

THREE

SAVAGE

FOURTEEN

"Here the sods come agen!" an excited Yorkshire voice yelled across the George V Dock. "Off the port bow! Nine of the Jerry sods!"

As Hull City's air-raid sirens started to sound once more, the off-duty ratings, dockers and port officials dashed for cover, while those of naval ships anchored in the basin, pulled on their anti-flash helmets and gloves and ran to their guns.

The Germans were trying their usual tactic. While the slow-flying Heinkels circled at height, trying to draw the city's anti-aircraft guns, a squadron of Focke-Wulf fighter bombers were coming in low, skimming up the estuary from the North Sea, going all out, knowing that they were well below the radar screen.

Bofors and pom-poms took up the challenge. Suddenly the sky above the Humber was peppered with black bursts of smoke. Still the German fighter-bombers came on. In an instant the morning air was hideous with the roar of the planes' engines, the thud-thud of the heavy flak and the frenetic, hysterical chatter of the quick-firers.

The first Focke-Wulfe came hurtling in at mast-top height. Just when it seemed it had to smack right into the water, the pilot pulled back his joystick. The big fighter-bomber surged into the sky trailing white smoke behind it. A myriad evil little black eggs tumbled from its blue-painted belly.

A freighter still out in the Humber was hit. It reeled as if it had been punched by a giant fist. Next moment it burst into flames from bow to stern. Panic-stricken seamen flung themselves into the water. Like a great fearsome blowtorch the searing flame caught them as they tried to escape. The water boiled and steamed. The steam rose and rose. When it dispersed there was no one there.

Another fighter-bomber came in. Its pilot weaved from side to side to put the gunners off their aim. Sometimes he yawed a good twenty feet to the left before doing the same to the right. He was obviously an expert. But Hull's gunners were used to the Germans' tricks of the trade. After all, the coastal city had suffered 3,000 raids since 1940. They coned the German, gradually getting closer to the Focke-Wulf. White angry flak streamed towards the plane.

It was hit. Oil streamed from the ruptured radial engine. Madly, the blinded pilot fought to keep control. To no avail. Suddenly the plane's nose dipped crazily. An instant later it plunged right into the Humber to the cheers of the sweating gunners.

Now the fighter-bombers split up, zooming in at masttop height to left and right, machineguns and cannon thumping away. The tracer ripping the lengths of their fuselages didn't deter the German pilots. They pressed home their attack with fanatical, reckless bravery.

A blinding flash. An oiler had been hit. It began to burn, sending up a pall of oily black smoke hundreds of feet into the grey morning sky. A moment later one of the attackers was struck, too. The pilot baled out.

Tracer ripped his chute cruelly to shreds. No mercy was ever given or expected in Hull. The pilot hurtled down like a ball to his death. He hit the deck of a destroyer and disintegrated like a pulpy, overripe scarlet fig.

Another freighter was hit. It broke in half almost immediately. Madly the crewmen dived into the estuary as the two halves reared up in gigantic fury, the screws churning the air purposely. Next instant the two parts had disappeared below the surface of the Humber leaving behind them two great bubbles of compressed air which exploded obscenely like two tremendous farts.

Now the fighter-bombers, those which had survived, were turning in tight controlled curves. They knew the British fighters at Linton-on-Ouse would have already been scrambled. Now they zoomed out over Spurn Head heading for the North Sea and their bases in Holland while the Heinkels continued to bomb, circling round the long-ruined smoking city below like metal hawks.

Captain Savage, DSO, DSC, placed another nitroglycerin tablet between his blue lips and under his tongue. The pain in his chest died almost immediately and he began to breathe easier as the last of the raiders fled. "I see what you mean, Fleming," he barked in that no-nonsense manner of his which had awed many a junior officer in years past. He tugged his battered cap to a more rakish angle and added, "The press might say the Hun has already lost the war, but those buggers don't seem to know that. They're attacking as if this was bloody 1940 and not 1944."

Fleming allowed himself a faint smile — no one would have dared to have smiled broadly in the tough old salt's presence — and said, "That's what we think in Room 39. They're definitely up to something in the Atlantic and we're hoping you're going to put a stop to it, sir."

"What me?" Savage exclaimed. "You know I'm on the sick list with my dickey ticker. I 'spect their Lordships will board me in the end. What use would I be to you, Fleming?"

"Well, sir, you do happen to be our best sub killer. Everyone knows that, sir, and, well, not to put too fine a point on it, we're dreadfully short of bodies."

"Scraping the bloody old barrel, what," Savage exclaimed as all about civilians and sailors came out of their hiding places to stare awe-struck at the heavy palls of dark smoke rising on all sides. Already the first ambulances were racing to the scene of the bombing, their bells jingling furiously.

A fire-engine rattled up, the firemen still wearing their pre-war burnished brass helmets, driven by a sweating driver in his undershirt with a Woodbine stuck in the corner of his mouth. Special constables, old men with the medal ribbons of the Old War on their burly chests, moved up and down the debris-littered streets waving their rattles and crying, "All clear ... all clear ... but don't you sailormen go down to them knocking shops in Hedon Road cos there's a ruddy great landmine down there which hasn't exploded!"

The ratings cheered hoarsely and Savage gave a wry painful grin, "Can't keep a matelot away from his women and rum, eh, Fleming?"

"Yessir," Fleming said dutifully as he steered the Captain to the waiting staff car, driven by a very pretty and smart Wren petty officer. She flung the two officers a tremendous salute which Savage returned a little wearily, for all swift physical movement seemed to hurt him these days. Watching the other man's hand tremble as he touched the rim of his peaked cap, Fleming realised for the first time that Savage was dying. All the same, he told himself, if anyone was going to stop the Hun it would be Captain Savage.

The car moved out into the sparse traffic and Fleming said, "The Admiral asked me to bring you up here sir to HMS *Drake* to have a look at the chaps in training and ask for volunteers for a new flotilla we're commissioning with you in command."

"Volunteers?" Savage echoed, looking out at the smoking ruins on all sides. Sweating Royal Engineers in gumboots and leather jerkins were digging deeper in a giant brown hole that looked like the work of some monstrous mole. Obviously there was an unexploded bomb down there somewhere. "Do matelots still volunteer after five years of war, Fleming?"

Fleming, who didn't know whether to take the remark as a joke or seriously, said, "Well, these chaps are still in their teens for the most part. That type is still usually keen."

"More scraping the barrel, eh. Well, get on with it, Fleming."

Hastily Fleming explained what he had learned from his agents in Lorient and from Bletchley about the German intentions. "We've guessed, sir, from what we now know, that the Boche are going to operate off the US coast. Kapitanleutnant Brandt will be in charge as far as I know."

"One Armed Brandt," Savage sat up suddenly very interested, his faded eyes abruptly bright and alert. "I've been trying to catch that bugger since '42 when he got among one of our convoys heading for Murmansk. Cunning bugger, sailed right beneath one of our merchantmen in the middle of the convoy so we couldn't get a proper sonar fix on him. Sank six ships before he did a bunk. But I nearly had him last year in the Med. Lost his left arm in that little affray. So they must be scraping the barrel, too, with a one-armed U-boat skipper." He gave Fleming a grin.

They passed a group of air-raid wardens, tin hats stuck at the back of their heads, hosing blood off the pavement. Near their feet there was a severed arm. Fleming looked away hastily and said, "Do you mind if I have a drink from my flask, sir? It's a Martini."

"Yes, I do, Fleming. We can't turn up smelling of drink. Now, let me ask you this: why can't the Yanks take care of this business themselves? Why should we look after their interests?"

Fleming, his long face a little sulky now, answered, "Because the PM wants us to have a high profile over there. He maintains that the Yanks are becoming the senior partner in the alliance, getting a little too big for their boots. He wants us to show them that we're still pretty good."

"A political thing, eh?" Savage dismissed the matter. "So my job is to attract enough volunteers to man four ships. Tall order you know, Fleming. Some of them won't even have been to sea and the North Atlantic in winter is no place for a matelot who hasn't yet found his sealegs. And all commanded by an officer who could die at any time!"

"Well, sir, that's the way their Lordships and naturally the PM, too, want it, sir."

Savage grinned again. "All right, Fleming, let's have that flask out now. I think I can stand a stiff 'un now." They rode the rest of the way to HMS *Drake* in silence.

The bugler raised his instrument to his lips and sounded the first note. Immediately the three divisions, Foretop, Maintop and Fo'c'sle, marched smartly onto the parade ground, six thousand young men swinging their arms smartly, watched by hard-eyed petty officers. Behind the sheds the band struck up. With a blare of brass it swung into sight, leading a guard with fixed bayonets marching towards the raised stand in front of the white ensign which fluttered in the wind.

Watching on the stand, Savage suddenly felt proud to belong to the Royal Navy, to be part of all this he saw in front of him. The band master barked an order. The band stopped playing and the trainee ratings formed up on parade.

The commodore in command standing at Savage's side raised his head and bellowed, "Parade stand at ease ... stand easy!" In the skeletal trees around the camp the rooks rose in hoarse cawing protest. The commodore yelled, "Captain Savage here, whose record as a destroyer captain with twelve known U-boat kills, speaks for itself, is going to ask for volunteers for immediate sea duty. All ratings from Class 16 B, the senior class, can volunteer their services if they wish. Now, then, listen carefully to what Captain Savage has to say."

Savage looked at the earnest young faces and thought the trainees were mere school kids. Aloud he said in that clipped bark of his, "Men, I want volunteers for a special mission. One which has been ordered by the Prime Minister himself. I can tell you nothing except that it will be dangerous probably and in the North Atlantic." He looked along their faces as if trying to etch their features on his mind's eye. "Any man of the Class 16 B who wishes to volunteer, one pace forward."

For a moment there was nothing save the sound of Savage's voice echoing and re-echoing around the barracks square. Then came the sharp click of a couple of hundred heels snapping together and booted feet taking that one pace forward.

"Good Gracious me," the commodore whispered to Fleming, "the whole ruddy lot, has volunteered!"

In front of them Savage's eyes suddenly filled with tears. Slowly he raised his gloved hand to his cap and said in a thick voice, "Men, I salute and thank you."

He swung round and faced the commodore, his eyes wet and said, "Commodore, have I your permission to lead off the Class of 16 B?"

The commodore snapped to attention and barked, "Why certainly, Captain Savage."

Fifteen minutes later the ratings were going were back in their Nissen huts, busily packing their kit, laughing and giggling like schoolboys released from a boring class at the end of the long day. They listened not to the doleful predictions of the three-stripers or ancient hookers with, "Never volunteer for nothin' in the Royal, chum. All yer'll get is a ruddy badge on yer arm with no pay", or "Go on, shipmate, volunteer and make a luvverly corpse." Or, "Cor stone the ferkin' crows, you lot need yer heads seeing to. Lash up and ferkin' stow — fancy volunteering!"

For they were going to war.

FIFTEEN

In the autumn of 1940 Savage, then still a lieutenant-commander, had gone slightly mad. He had flown back from the Med on leave and taken the train to Portsmouth which was in the middle of a savage air-raid. Somehow he had found a taxi driver to take him out to his home at Southsea, arriving with the sirens beginning to sound the all clear.

North Street had almost vanished. He had pushed his way past the struggling, sweating rescue workers, hacking away at the smouldering ruins and had found them all dead: Alice, his wife, was naked in a bath of her own blood. There seemed not a mark on her delightful nude body, but she was dead all right; he had seen enough dead in the last year to know that. Betsy, his fourteen-year-old daughter had vanished altogether. Her body was never found. John, his naval cadet son, on leave from Dartmouth to meet his father, he found himself: in pieces hanging from a shattered tree in what had been their garden, like some monstrous human red-pulped fruit.

The doctors had pumped him full of dope for forty-eight hours which had finally stopped his howling and raving. Then he had buried them with the wind howling in from the Channel and fluttering the naval chaplain's surplice, drowning his soothing words. Not that he would have listened to them anyway; for in his mind there was only one word going round and round like a gramophone record; *Kill ... kill ... kill."*

He had gone straight back to his destroyer in the Med. That month he had sunk two submarines — one Italian and one German. When his first officer had asked for permission to rescue the survivors he had snapped brutally, "No, let the bastards die ... They don't deserve to live."

Jimmy the One had looked aghast. "But, sir," he had protested, "it's only fair to rescue —"

"There's nothing fair about this war, Number One," he had cut in brutally. "I've got a good mind to shoot the bastards now."

After Crete, when Mountbatten had been sunk in 1941, he had taken over the playboy's flotilla and pursued the enemy with relentless, cold-blooded fury. Twice he was mentioned by name by Lord Haw-Haw as, "that English butcher who doesn't hesitate to shoot helpless German seamen in the water against all the rules of decency and land warfare."

In 1942, old Admiral ABC Cunningham, the commander-in-chief in the Mediterranean, had summoned him to his headquarters in Alexandria and said, "Now, listen Savage, you're overdoing it. You've been at sea for eighty-four consecutive days. I know on reliable information that at least one of your destroyer skippers is on the verge of a nervous breakdown."

Savage had looked down at old "ABC", as he was called on account of his initials throughout the fleet and had said stonily, "Give me the man's name, sir, and I'll replace him immediately."

"That's not the point, Savage," ABC had snapped. "You've sunk an Eyetie cruiser, shot up two of Rommel's convoys for North Africa and I hear you got so close to the Greek coast that you were able to knock out a German troop train heading for Salonica! You can't keep it up, you know. Go on like this and it will be *you* who has the nervous breakdown."

"Is that all, sir?" he had asked, his thin taut face expressionless.

ABC had dismissed him with an angry wave of his old hand and he had taken his flotilla straight back to sea again.

When the end came in North Africa he had personally manned a machinegun on his own ship and blasted a boatload of panic-stricken Afrika Korps troopers out of the water, killing the lot of them with cold-blooded, calculating brutality. For days afterwards the crew had avoided looking at him, walking by him with their eyes averted; and meals were eaten in the wardroom in silence.

He hadn't cared. He had taken his flotilla into the invasion of Sicily, the landings at Salerno and Anzio, where he had gone ashore personally at the time of a threatened German breakthrough to the beaches and set up a provisional naval battalion from his crews. When the Guards broke and started streaming back to the beaches he had personally shot two of them and forced them back to their positions. They went reluctantly muttering, "Yon officer's a madman," a view shared now by most of Savage's officers and sailors.

Summoned back to England to receive his DSO and DSC from King George he had been told later by Pound, the head of the Admiralty, "Savage, you've got to stop this. I know you are a very brave man and undoubtedly our best destroyer leader, but you're killing yourself, man. You've got to rest!"

"I'll rest, sir," he had replied, unable to stop the little nervous tic on the left side of his face, "when this war is over and there are no more Boche to kill."

He had gone back to sea. He had taken part in the D-Day landings, ramming a couple of mini-submarines which had managed to penetrate the destroyer screen and shooting the skipper of one forced to the surface who refused to surrender. Then he had been transferred to the Murmansk run when it had happened.

They were just off Bear Island, escorting a slow convoy of merchantmen laden with tanks for the Russians, when a German cruiser made its appearance, firing at the ships from a range of eight or nine miles. Savage took up the challenge at once. Leaving the rest of the flotilla to guard the merchantmen he sailed alone to fight the far larger German cruiser.

Shells bracketed the little destroyer almost immediately. Great gouts of whirling white water spurted up on either side of the sleek rakish craft. At his side his Number One yelled, "Let's stick a couple of tin fish at her from this range, sir!"

"No," Savage replied firmly, holding onto his steel helmet as the destroyer reeled under another near miss with tons of water pouring over her stern. "I'm taking no chances, Number One. I want a visual target before I launch my torp —"

"There she is, sir!" one of the lookouts sang out. "Bearing Red."

The two officers swung up their glasses as one. A long grey shape was emerging from the seafog, its nine heavy guns in three turrets poised to fire again, the crooked cross banner streaming from her stern.

"God save me, what a big bastard," his Number One exclaimed. "She must be at least ten thousand tons."

"The bigger they are the harder they fall!" Savage made a quick decision. He knew there was no time for long deliberations. "Bring her round," he commanded yelling out the bearing. "Prepare to fire one and two."

The cruiser fired again. The destroyer reeled as shells landed close by. Shrapnel hissed everywhere. A signaller went down, his severed arm landing on the deck before him. The wireless mast came tumbling down, trailing angry blue sparks after it. Then they were surging forward at thirty knots, cleaving the water, sending up a curve of wild white water at the ship's bows. Their own guns began firing. On the deck of the cruiser the gunners manned their quick firers. A hail of shot and shell streamed towards the attacker.

"Three thousand ... two fifty ... two thousand ... " Number One counted off the range as the torpedo men waited for the order to fire. "One thousand five hundred!"

Savage knew he could wait no longer. Their luck wouldn't hold out much more. "Fire one ... fire two ..." he yelled at the top of his voice. *"Fire!"*

The two torpedoes leapt from the launcher. They hit the water in a flurry of bubbles. Next moment they were speeding towards the German cruiser.

Savage flashed a look at his wristwatch checking the running time. Two seconds passed, three, suddenly the cruiser shook violently as if punched by an invisible fist. A series of little scarlet flashes ran the length of the ship. There was a tremendous roar. Next instant she broke in two and the water was suddenly filled with heads as men splashed and choked and fought, desperately trying to get away from their ship before she went under.

"Hell's teeth," the first officer yelled in sheer amazed delight. "We've done it! We've sunk the bugger" He stopped short and his look of delight changed to one of great concern. "Sir," he exclaimed, "are you all right?" Savage's face had gone an ashen white. In a matter of moments he seemed to have aged ten years. "Sir!"

Savage felt a merciless stab of pain in his chest. He reached out a hand to steady himself. Too late. Next instant all had gone black and he found himself falling.

Two weeks later the surgeon-lieutenant at Haslar told him, "Fraid you've overdone it for too long, Captain. Your heart has been strained beyond repair."

Savage looked up at him. "Do you mean you're going to put me out to grass?"

"That's not my job, Captain," the surgeon-lieutenant said. "All I can say is that if you take it easy, a lot easier, you can live to be a hundred. What happens to your career is up to the Board."

Savage, weak as he still was, was unable to restrain that sharp temper of his. "But dammit, man. I have no other life than the Navy. I've been in the service since I was thirteen. I can't pretend to be a bloody farmer and Tory member of the local bloody council. I know nothing else but ships and battle." He looked at the doctor, faded eyes blazing.

The surgeon-lieutenant had said nothing but, "That'll be up to the Board, Captain," and left.

Now Savage was being offered one last chance, thanks to the Prime Minister.

"With permission, sir, you're a damned fool to accept," the surgeon-lieutenant said when he told him he had accepted Fleming's offer. "The slightest bit of strain, excitement, danger could kill you like that." He clicked his fingers sharply. "You're a sick man, you should know that." He pointed to the ribbons on Savage's tunic. "You've done your bit, and more. Let someone else have a go." Then when he saw that his words were having no effect on Savage he cried in desperation, "Do you *want* to die?"

Savage looked up at his angry young face and answered in a quiet voice, "Yes."

Now as the train carrying him and his young recruits hurried southwards towards Harwich, he told himself he didn't want to die, just yet. He had to knock them into shape quickly and be underway to stop whatever the Boche had in mind off the American East Coast. It was a challenge again. He had a job to do once more.

Suddenly, perhaps for the first time since the autumn of 1940, Captain Savage was a little happy.

His teenage ratings were happy, too, if apprehensive. Packed in the third class compartments with the fading pre-war posters for "Bracing Bridlington" and "Come to Saucy Scarborough," their kits bulging from the nettings above them, they played "housey-housey", smoked Woodbines incessantly and, in the manner of all sailors passed on the latest "Buzzes". "We're off East," they said, "cos that old hooker in stores said they were indenting for tropical whites."

"Garn," they answered, "pull the other one. It's got frigging bells on it. We're not going to no East. We're off to Holland. Gonna invade the Dutch coast. I know for certain because they're issuing Dutch phrase books as soon as we get to Harwich. A writer in bay told me it, but I had to keep it under me hat."

"A proper lash-up!" they said. "Who the frig would use old Savage for the invasion o' Holland? Not on yer nelly. I know for certain that old Jerry's got a new type of U-boat. Savage is gonna try and nab one so them boffins in the Admiralty can find out its secrets. The Jerries is supposed to run them on something called atoms, whatever they is when they're at home."

But despite their apparent cynicism they were excited. It was going to be an adventure. They were going on active service. Most of them had been through the Blitz. They had seen their homes destroyed. Back in the bad days when the U-boats had almost brought Britain to its knees they had lived off pathetic scraps of meat and mouldy old potatoes and powdered egg. Now it was different. They were going to pay Old Jerry back for what he had done through the years when they had been growing up. "If old Savage is running this little lot," they chortled happily, "then Jerry's gonna cop a real frigging packet."

SIXTEEN

Everything was frenzied activity at Lorient. Inside the heavily guarded submarine pens all was hurrying sailors, supply trucks and horse-drawn carts bringing up the ammunition, stores, food and a hundred and one things the Brandt Wolf Pack would need for the great surprise attack.

Mountains of canned food disappeared into the maws of the four boats drawn up in floodlit pens. They were not the usual cans of "old man", tinned meat reputedly made from dead old men collected from Berlin's many workhouses. These were the kind of delicacies that Lorient's beleaguered garrison, where half the bread was made up of sawdust, hadn't seen for many a day. There was canned French butter, finest sausages and even real bean coffee made from coffee beans not acorns. As Brandt hurrying about his duties heard one awed rating say, "Holy strawsack, they'll be loading caviar next!"

To which a sour-faced petty officer who had grown old in the service replied miserably, "Yer, they allus fatten us up before they give us the chop. This one is an Ascension Day commando, if there ever was one."

Brandt nodded his head slightly as if in agreement. He knew better than most that this was going to be a one way ticket to heaven or hell. The Brandt Wolf Pack wouldn't be coming back from this particular wartime patrol.

On the day before the Schulze Group — it had been delayed due to bad weather — sailed, the E-boats brought in the V-2 parts. Hurriedly the sweating dockers and naval engineers started to assemble them in front of the wide-eyed submariners. All of them had by now seen the newsreels of the V-2 attacks and it didn't take long for them to recognise what they were. The buzzes started immediately.

Brandt knew he must stop them at once. With his empty sleeve tucked into his belt, for they had not yet flown him in another wooden arm, he had the crews assembled that same afternoon. "Now, comrades," he barked above the howl of the wind coming straight off the Atlantic and the noise of the docks, "I know you've heard the buzz that we're sailing with those missiles and the buzz is right. But by the Great God and All His Seven Triangles, I'll have the eggs off'n any sailor here who says I told you so, with a blunt razor!"

The young submariners, their bell bottoms rippling about their legs in the stiff breeze, laughed. He knew the "blue boys" appreciated a little bit of salty language from their commanders.

"It will be a dangerous mission. But the risk will be worth it. If we succeed it might mean a turning point in the war and final victory for our beloved Fatherland." His gaze hardened and he looked along their ranks with such intensity that one or two of the younger sailors shuddered involuntarily at the utter ruthlessness of that searing gaze.

"At seventeen hundred hours this day I am going to stand you all down. You've done as much as you can by now. The rest will be up to the dockers and engineers. For you it is to be party time on the express orders of the Big Lion," Brandt meant Grossadmiral Doenitz. "There'll be a bottle of Frog brandy per man, as much wine and suds as you can drink and mountains of sauerkraut and good German sausage." There was a cheer at his announcement and here and there sailors licked their lips in anticipation after the starvation rations most of them had lived on ever since they had reached Lorient.

Brandt held up his hand for silence. "This night Wolf Pack Brandt gets blind-drunk." His command "dismiss" was drowned by the sailors' cheers and hurrahs, and cries of *"Es lebe Gruppe Brandt* ... Long live Brandt Group!"

As they streamed away back to their tasks, Brandt's grin vanished. "Long Live Brandt Group," he muttered to himself. How long, though, he wondered. They were all lambs being led to the slaughter. He dismissed that gloomy thought and walked over to his office.

Leutnant Schulze, the head of the sabotage group, was waiting for him. He clicked his heels together in a not very military fashion. "Leutnant Schulze zur Stelle. Herr Kapitanleutnant!" His right arm flicked up in the Hitler salute.

Brandt looked at him coldly, touched his cap in a careless manner and said, "Sit down, Lieutenant."

He did the same and looked at the other man. He was not impressed. Schulze was small and a little chubby. His face was greasy and he kept running his tongue around his fat bright red bottom lip. He looked like a man who sweated a lot.

"You know the latest order from Obersturmbannfuhrer Skorzeny?" Brandt said.

"Yes sir and we sail on the night tide."

"Yes, I've already discussed that with Lieutenant Heims, the 1220 commander. He's young but experienced. What I want to talk to you about is security. There can be no slip-ups. Your men will have to be in position at precisely the time the attack starts. I think my chaps have only a twenty five per cent chance of surviving the attack so the shorter the time we're off the American coast the better. Target, launch and run for it, that's the order of the day."

"There will be no slip-ups, sir," Schulze said earnestly, running his tongue over his bottom lip once again. "All my men know New York City intimately, that's why they were picked. I myself worked in the Hotel Taft for seven years."

"As a waiter, I've read your record," Brandt cut him off sharply.

"Why, yes, sir," Schulze answered, somewhat deflated.

"To continue," Brandt said trying to overcome his dislike of the former waiter: there was something unwholesome about him but he couldn't put his finger on it. "We have sent missions to the United States before. In 1942, for instance. That group of twelve men was betrayed by greed and treachery." He stared hard at the other man. "You must stamp out any treachery with complete ruthlessness, do you understand? Not only does your own life depend upon it but also those of my young 'blue boys'."

"I understand, sir," Schulze said promptly, but to Brandt he seemed to be avoiding his gaze.

"All right then," Brandt rose to his feet and offered his hand. "I'd like to wish you success."

"Thank you, sir." Schulze took his hand.

Brandt repressed a shudder with difficulty. Schulze's hand was soft and moist. It didn't feel pleasant at all. He withdrew his grip hurriedly and said, "I shall come and see your people off on the night tide. Till then. And remember what I said, Schulze. You are to be completely ruthless with traitors."

"Yessir," Schulze saluted and went out leaving Brandt alone with his thoughts.

They weren't particularly pleasant. He thought about Gerda for while and realised he would never see her again. She would probably languish in a French prison for a while. But she wouldn't talk about her job in Nordhausen and her relationship with him or who he was. He trusted her implicitly. In the end she would be released and he hoped that she could find some happiness eventually. But he knew that there was no hope of his ever seeing her again. The die had been cast. He was caught up in this suicide mission whether he liked it or not. There was no turning back.

For a while his mind went blank. In a dream, as it grew gradually darker outside, he was vaguely aware of the clatter of machinery, the cries of the gulls picking up scraps from the oily water, the bellows of the petty officers as they stood the submariners down: all the old familiar sounds of docks which had been part and parcel of his life since he had been a young cadet.

Suddenly, for no reason in particular, he was cheerful again. Perhaps it was the sounds reminding him once again of the old cheerful, happy-go-lucky camaraderie of sailors. They led a tough hard life, facing all kinds of danger, natural as well as manmade; yet they always seemed to be laughing, whistling or cracking dirty jokes. Maybe it was a protective cover but it got them through the day. He smiled at himself in the mirror on the opposite wall of his office and then nodded with approval at the face he saw there: hard, lean and confident, the eyes smiling but wary, very wary. "Brandt, he said to himself in the fashion of lonely men, "you're going to hang one on tonight, a real skinful. Who knows, it might be your last chance." Cheerfully he winked at his image and reached for his hat.

Already the Wolf Pack's boozy evening had degenerated into a drunken orgy. The noise was tremendous. The big hall shook with the noise. Drunken sailors bawled off key at the top of their voices drowning the attempts of the blonde French chanteuse, with her red dress slit to the thigh to reveal she wore nothing underneath.

There were drunken unconscious U-boat men everywhere, lying with their heads in puddles of suds, snoring, sprawled out on the floor oblivious to the stumbling feet that crossed their bodies. There was even one petty officer hanging from his collar from a hat stand, snoring merrily.

Of course there were plenty of women, drinking champagne out of the bottle, sitting on sailors' knees and letting them fondle their naked breasts. There was even a couple underneath one of the bottle-littered tables going at it, the rest of the room forgotten in their urgent need.

Brandt sat in the corner smoking a cigar, drinking his usual *lutt un' lutt,* a small glass of clear schnapps drunk straight down, followed by a small beer chaser. He had ordered the harassed French steward in a beer-stained white tunic to line up six of them on the table as soon as he had arrived. Already he was down to two.

His companion was the Wolf Pack's medical officer, "The Pox Doctor" as he was universally known in the Pack; Professor Hermann Hartung, lately professor of sexually transmitted diseases at Berlin University. As he had said when he first reported to Brandt, "Herr Kapitanleutnant, I think I shall see more varieties of VD than we academics in our ivory towers have ever dreamed of." Three years later he would often confess in the mess, *"Meine Herren,* never have I seen such exotic varieties of syphilis as I have encountered with our Wolf Pack. I do declare that if I survive this war I shall write a classic text entitled *Sex and the Single Sailor,* which always occasioned a burst of somewhat apprehensive laughter.

But tonight the Pox Doctor was not worried. "All their yellow cards," he meant the medical certificates of the whores who were now ripping off what was left of their scant clothing for the mass orgy soon to come, "are signed, sealed and bang up-to-date," he stated. "Certified fit for human consumption, even Lola there." He indicated a big bosomed blonde who wasn't a natural blonde, Brandt could see that, and who now lay naked on a sopping table with her legs spread wide apart crying drunkenly *"Vite allemands, sie wollen fickificki?"*

"I hope she doesn't catch her death of cold with her legs spread like that, poor dear." Brandt opined as the drunken sailors jostled and pushed each other wildly in their attempts to jump upon the nubile dyed blonde.

"No, my dear fellow," the Pox Doctor said, "I don't think Lola will die of that exactly. Hello," his cultured intelligent face behind the gold pince-nez he affected grew suddenly thoughtful.

"What is it?" Brandt asked putting down his glass.

Hartung pointed to one of the waiters, a handsome Frenchman with a very large clubfoot who was standing in the corner, a sulky look on his face, looking at the high jinks all around. "I caught that feller four weeks ago with Leutnant Schulze, you know him?"

Brandt nodded, "Yes."

"Well, he suffered an unfortunate affliction which I managed to catch with Salvarsan in its early stages. You know these chaps are supposed to report when they think they got VD. But Schulze gave me a devil of a time before he finally spat it out. I had to promise him on my doctor's oath not to reveal anything —" He broke off.

Brandt, as drunk as he was, stared at him aghast. "You mean Schulze and the Frenchman? I mean is Schulze that way ... a warm brother?"

The Pox Doctor nodded. "He certainly is. To judge by certain parts of his anatomy he has been one for several years."

"Grosser Gott im Himmel!" Brandt cursed, "and he's in charge of the targeting party!" He flashed a look at his watch and groaned again. He had completely forgotten the night tide. The U-boat with Schulze on board had already sailed.

Hartung read his thoughts. "If you think he is a danger to the mission, old house, can't you wireless the U-boat and have it recalled?"

Brandt shook his head. "Impossible. It's operational now and under orders not to break radio silence for another forty-eight hours until it's well out into the Atlantic. It's standard operating procedure so that the Tommies, who are always lurking off submarine bases, can't get a fix on the craft."

"What can you do then?"

"This. Arrest that little warm brother with the funny foot. At least through him we can find out more about our dear friend Leutnant Schulze. Come on, Hartung."

The waiter saw them pushing their way through the crowd of drunken sailors and screeching whores. He must have known instinctively that they were going to arrest him. He raised his arm. The tray laden with filled glasses came flying towards them. Glass cracked and broke everywhere. A sailor yelled, "Hey, the Frogs have revolted. Mutiny!"

"Mutiny," someone else yelled. "The crew of frigging 1225 have frigging mutinied!"

"Trust those frigging perverted banana-suckers. At them, mates!"

In an instant the big room erupted into an all-out fist fight. Sailors were going at each other with fists, bottles and chair legs. The big mirror behind the bar splintered. A sailor slipped in dodging a punch and gripping the chanteuse's red silk dress pulled it off to reveal she was completely naked beneath it. "Frigging impudence," she shrieked and kicked the sailor with her high-heeled shoe. "No respect for a frigging lady!" He went reeling back clutching a broken nose.

Brandt, suddenly very sober, hesitated no longer. He pulled out his pistol and fired three shots into the ceiling. "Stop that," he bellowed. "Stop that at once!"

As abruptly as it had started the brawl ended. Men swayed, looking sheepishly at each other. Bottles and chair legs clattered to the debris-littered floor. The band started up again somewhat raggedly and the chanteuse, still wearing only high heels, launched into a shaky version of *J'attendrai.*

Brandt pointed his still smoking pistol at the club-footed waiter. *"Allez, vite,"* he commanded quietly. *"Kommen Sie mit!"*

His shoulders slumped in defeat, the waiter did as he was commanded.

SEVENTEEN

The cop swung the broom handle with all his might. It twacked with a tremendous blow against the pail placed over the prisoner's head. He reeled, but the stout ropes with which they had bound him to the chair kept him firmly in place.

Brandt, drawing on his cigar, lounging at the wall of the Gestapo cellar in the faint yellow light flinched. He could just imagine what the effect of that blow would be inside the pail. The poor little queer would be bleeding at nostrils and ears, virtually deafened.

Next to him Diels, the local Gestapo chief, fat, complacent and as usual dressed in a felt hat with the brim pulled well down his dark eyes and a creaking leather coat which reached to his ankles said, "I've been known to make a mummy talk, Herr Kapitanleutnant." He chuckled at his own humour. "But some of these warm brothers are very tough, especially when their lovers are involved. You wouldn't think it with their frigging limp wrists and fake voices, but they are."

Thwack! the sweating cop, stripped to the waist to reveal his bulging muscles, slammed the broom handle against the pail once again. Brandt thought he heard a muffled scream. He said, "Don't you think he's had enough, Kommissar?"

"Soon," the Gestapo man said easily. "Give him another couple of whacks and then he'll be ripe, I have no doubt. The trick in this kind of business," he went on as the sweating, half-naked cop raised his broom handle once again, "is not to be half-hearted. If you're going to hit 'em, hit 'em hard I allus say."

The cop slammed the broom handle against the pail yet again. Now blood started to pour from it onto the tied man's chest. Brandt shook his head in mock wonder. Why hadn't the warm brother spoken up right from the start, then he would have been spared all this unnecessary misery?" They were going to shoot him as a spy and a homosexual at dawn anyway.

"Course, I oughtn't to be doing this now," the Kommissar said and yawned in a bored fashion as if he had seen it all before, and then some. "I'm due for my pension next year. Thirty years a cop. If I'm caught when we surrender here the Frogs'll send me up the chimney." With a fat finger like a hairy pork sausage he made the gesture of rising smoke. "No doubt about that and where will my pension be then eh?"

Thwack! Again the broom handle smacked the side of the pail. The blood flowed even more. The Kommissar took the cigar out of his mouth lazily and said, "All right, Otto, that should have about done him." He said the words as if he were talking about a pan of meat.

"Jawohl, Herr Kommissar," the cop panted. He spat in his big hands which were flushed crimson with the effort of beating the prisoner and removed the pail.

Brandt gave a little gasp. He hardly recognised the handsome waiter of half an hour before when he had first refused to speak. His eyes were puffed to narrow slits, blood was streaming from thickened nostrils and ears, and his cheeks were a mess of congealed blood and dark bruises. He groaned and let his head fall on his chest as if he were infinitely weary.

"Wake him up, Otto," the Kommissar commanded.

"Jawohl, Herr Kommissar," the cop replied woodenly. He went into the corner of the cellar where there was a tap, dutifully rinsed the blood from inside the pail and filled it to the brim with water. He placed himself in front of the prisoner and then slung the contents at his face.

The waiter jerked, sat up, groaned and tried to open his eyes wider. *"Sale con,"* he said weakly but defiantly through his hugely swollen, cracked lips.

Evidently the Kommissar understood some French for he said easily, "I know I am. I've been a dirty cunt all my life. Now, then, just answer a couple of questions and we'll let you get some shuteye." It was the voice of sweet reason itself, not the harsh bullying shouting tone he had adopted when he had first attempted to question the prisoner. Brandt could see that the fat Gestapo man had been at the business a long time. He knew his awful trade.

The prisoner hawked drily and spat on the dirty floor of the cellar.

Routinely the Gestapo man slapped him across the face sending his head flying to the left. "Nasty," he said like a mother rebuking a naughty child. "Shouldn't do that if I were you. I could be very unpleasant if I wanted to. You've had certain pleasant things up your arse in your time, no doubt. I could shove something very unpleasant up that hole without the benefit of vaseline either." He coughed, shielding his open mouth delicately. "Now, then, we know you've been having a bit of the old two-backed beast with Leutnant Schulze. No harm in that. Each man to his own taste, I say. I'm no spoilsport. Used to know a lot of pavement boys," he meant male prostitutes, "in Berlin before the war. Nice chaps most of them. Allus pretty good with their backhanders to the cops." He made the gesture of counting money. "All we want to know is what Leutnant Schulze told you about his mission and what you passed on to the Tommies."

The prisoner opened his mouth as if to protest but the Gestapo man beat him to it. "No use trying to get out of it, old house. We found the messages in code in the heel of your surgical boot. We Boche," he emphasised the term of contempt, "are not so foolish as you Frogs think we are."

He waited. Brandt stubbed out his cigar impatiently. Why didn't the queer bastard spit it out, he asked himself and get it over with? He felt sorry for him in a way but the lives of his young crews came first.

Kommissar Diels noted the impatient gesture. Out of the side of his broad mouth, not taking his ferret eyes off the battered prisoner for one moment, he said, *"Alles mit der Ruhe, Herr Kapitanleutnant.* Easy does it."

Brandt nodded his understanding.

The Gestapo man opened up his heavy leather coat. It creaked quite noisily as he did so. He unclipped the thick long rubber truncheon from his belt. On the other side of the cellar the cop grinned. He said, "That'll put him off the other for a long time, Herr Kommissar."

"Spect it will," the Kommissar thrust the black rubber truncheon through a circle formed by his thumb and forefinger slowly, suggestively.

The prisoner's battered face contorted into a look of horror. "I don't ... go in for that kind of thing," he stuttered in good German.

The Kommissar's grin broadened. "Then you're going to lose your virginity, without the benefit of vaseline. Otto, rip his pants off at once!" he bellowed suddenly. Otto stepped forward, hands outstretched.

The prisoner shrank back and screamed in panic, "All right, all right, I'll tell you what you want to know."

The Kommissar nodded to the cop who looked disappointed and said to Brandt, "Am I authorised to hear this?"

"Yes, but send him out," Brandt indicated the other cop.

"All right, Otto, fart into the wind."

Otto looked disappointed but he went pulling on his shirt and muttering to himself.

The Kommissar waited till he'd gone. Then he said, "That Otto's all muscle. Nothing in the head though. Good to have gotten rid of him. A sniff at the barmaid's apron and he'd be talking his head off. No keeping secrets with Otto." He turned to the prisoner, "All right, son," he said in an almost kindly fashion. "Let's be having it now, *dalli, dalli,* what did your dear lieutenant tell you?"

"He was going to America," the prisoner said, tears suddenly running down his ruined face as if he had realised for the first time there was no hope for him. "He was to sabotage or spy there."

"Did he say where?" Brandt rapped swiftly.

"No, no."

"Come on, no lying now," the Kommissar said thrusting the thick black rubber club between his fingers threateningly.

"I'm not. All he said was America, no more. I swear to you that," the waiter stammered brokenly, the tears streaming down his cheeks.

"And what did you do with that information?" the Kommissar asked.

The man looked at his feet as if he knew he was condemning himself to death by his own words. "I passed it to someone who came in for the black market. He, she, knew a way through your lines. They took what I knew."

"To whom?"

"The English ..." the man's voice trailed away to nothing for he knew there was no more to be said. He had told them all they needed to know.

The Kommissar looked pointedly at Brandt. The latter shook his head. He'd had enough. The Kommissar raised his voice. "All right, Otto, come on in and take this scallywag away. See he gets a slug of firewater and a cancer stick. He's going to need them."

Half an hour later Brandt was on the phone to Skorzeny in his remote German HQ. The SS leader was plainly disgruntled at having been dragged out of his bed in the small hours of the morning and when Brandt said, "Shall we scramble?" he said grumpily, "All right, get on with it. Where's the fire?"

Swiftly, knowing that the Allied listeners outside Lorient would be tapping the cable, sweating to unscramble the conversation, Brandt told Skorzeny what they had learned from the waiter.

Skorzeny listened without interruption then said, "Great crap on the Christmas tree, that's shitting good news isn't it. I ask you!"

Brandt said nothing. At the other end of the line he could imagine the scarfaced giant's thoughts racing as he tried to come to terms with the new situation. Finally Skorzeny said, "So the Tommies know that we are sending a U-boat to the USA filled with saboteurs. But they don't know why, agreed?"

"Agreed."

"They'll only know when they capture this warm brother, what's the swine's name?"

"Schulze."

"Yes, Schulze, when they capture him and he starts spilling his guts. Those perverts have got no stamina or loyalty." Brandt thought of the poor wretched waiter who would soon die but said nothing. "Then they'll know, but not before."

"Yes, I suppose so," Brandt admitted wondering where this was leading. "But there is nothing we can do about that now. The U-boat with his team is underway. It'll take another forty-eight hours before we can recall her."

"But we won't."

"Won't what?"

"Recall her," Skorzeny answered his voice suddenly full of cunning and silky Viennese charm.

"What do you mean?"

"We'll let her carry on until she is in American air space. Then we'll ask her skipper to report his position. That position we'll radio to Berlin, in clear."

"In clear?" Brandt echoed foolishly staring at the wall puzzled. "But why in clear?" That will give the U-boat's position away to the enemy immediately. They listen to all our signals just as we do to theirs."

"Exactly," Skorzeny said smoothly. "The Amis'll send their planes out immediately. The U-boat won't have a chance. The Amis'll bomb all hell out of it and Messrs Schulze and Co will go to the bottom of the Atlantic Ocean and that particular problem will be solved." Skorzeny sounded very pleased with himself at this easy solution.

"But that will be plain bloody murder, Obersturmbannfuhrer!" Brandt cried aghast. "Perhaps Schulze deserves to die for giving away that information to the Frenchman. But the others don't, the U-boat crew, I mean. They are honest, decent German sailors, risking their lives for the Fatherland."

"I understand all that, Brandt," Skorzeny said soothingly. "It's a shame, I admit, but you can't make an omelette without breaking eggs."

"This is no shitting omelette, Skorzeny!" Brandt yelled into the phone, face flushed crimson with rage. "We're talking about boys, mere boys. You just can't tell me that you will order their deaths just like that?" He gasped, unable to continue, barely capable of believing what he had just heard.

"Orders are orders, Brandt!" Skorzeny rasped harshly, sudden menace in his voice. "We cannot afford to risk the success of the whole operation on account of the lives of a handful of teenage seamen. The future of the Homeland is at stake whether we win or lose this damned war. That overrules all other considerations."

"But —"

"There are no buts. Just carry out your orders as planned. That is all."

Suddenly the line went dead. Skorzeny had hung up.

Now Brandt was stone cold sober. He stared at the phone numbly. There was no sound save the steady tramp of the sentry's boots on the gravel outside and the hiss of the wind from the sea. What kind of a country was he serving, he asked himself. For five years he had done his best, risking his life over and over again, losing an arm for the cause. Then there had been Nordhausen and Gerda; now this. Could he still continue to fight for a regime which had absolutely no respect for the individual and sacrificed them brutally, even mindlessly? "What am I to do?" he asked. "Please tell me what am I to do?" But no answer came to that overwhelming question.

EIGHTEEN

"'Ome, 'ome sweet 'ome, sir," the wizened old chief petty officer said.

Savage touched his hand to his battered cap and ducked as he entered the long narrow ship's room. It was lined with bunks and hammocks and lit by a single electric bulb. It stank of diesel oil, damp metal and human sweat. Someone had just farted and it stank of that, too. The only furniture was a long metal mess table a wasteland of dirty chipped enamel mugs and plates with a big yellow tin of plum jam in the centre from which protruded a dirty long carving knife.

"Well, I've seen worse," Savage said not even noticing the smell.

The old chief petty office pulled a face and Savage knew he was expected to be shocked so he said, pointing to half a loaf of white bread turning soggy from the puddle of spilled tea in which it rested, "Very wasteful, chiefie. Can't have the men wasting good bread like that. Next time you see anything like that get some names for the rattle."

The old CPO brightened up. He was the old sort who were never happier than when they were putting some unfortunate seaman on report. "The rattle. Ay ay, sir," he snapped with alacrity. "You'll be wanting to look at the heads now, sir, won't yer?"

Savage nodded, though he didn't want to see the ship's lavatories. His chest was hurting again and he was feeling a little sick. All the same he was glad to be back at sea once more and feel that he had already come to grips with these mixed crews of old petty officers who would have been long retired if there hadn't been war and young ratings on active service for the first time.

They walked down the companionway, young ratings squeezing themselves against the metal walls as they passed and trying to salute at the same time.

"The ablutions, sir," the CPO barked indicating the line of zinc bowls set in holes the length of a wooden table, all thick with the scum of shaving soap. "And there's the heads." He pointed to the line of lavatories without doors. "We try to stop them from freezing by pouring hot water down 'em at regular intervals. That kettle over there is on the boil all the time, but most of them young ratings when they come off watch just make themsens a cup o' char."

Savage surveyed the lavatories with their usual collection of crude drawings symbolising a sailor's sexual fantasies and the old bit of doggerel maintaining, *"It's no use standing on the seat, the crabs in this place jump six feet,"* and told himself that the life the officers lived in the wardroom was a world apart from that of the ratings. How could they stand such conditions and still carry out their hard, back-breaking duties?

He nodded and said as he expected the CPO wanted him to say, "Not particularly Bristol fashion, chiefie. Get 'em to clean it up a bit."

"I thought you'd say that, sir. I'll chase 'em up, don't you worry, sir."

Savage smiled to himself. The wizened old petty officer would now use him to frighten the young ratings. It would be, "The Skipper said" and "The Skipper told me to tell you lot of lazy baskets ..."

"Dishing out the rum ration, sir, now. Better have a look, don't yer think, sir?"

Suppressing the bile that was flooding his throat Savage nodded. "Yes, of course, chiefie."

Together they threaded their way back through the maze of corridors to the mess deck where, under the supervision of the Officer of the Day, the leading seaman of each mess was carefully measuring out a tot of rum to each member of his mess who "drew".

Savage watched as the leading seamen took a taste of each tot. They were entitled to their "sippers" as they were known and

Savage guessed it was a custom that went back to before Nelson's time. Indeed, rum was the principal currency of the lower deck, he knew that. If you did a man a favour he might offer you a "lighter" a mere wetting of the lips with rum. A slightly bigger favour might get you a "sipper" and a really big favour might entitle you to a "gulper", which meant the recipient could gulp down the whole tot.

The thought made Savage forget his pain, even made him feel a little happy. Again he was reminded of how long he had been in the Royal Navy and how much he loved this hard but simple life. He could not visualise any other kind. He could not even contemplate a life in civvie street. His smile vanished and he frowned as one of the leading hands enjoyed a "gulper", he must have done a very great favour for the rating who had given it to him. What was going to happen to that man, he asked himself, after this cruise?

Their Lordships were hard realistic men. Once he had done what they wanted of him he knew that would be that. They'd get rid of him, send him off to grass with a meagre pension. That would be that. Captain Savage become Mr Savage, complete with bowler hat.

"Sir," a frightened voice broke into his reverie. Startled, Savage swung round. An ashen-faced rating in a duffel coat, his face wet with spray, stood gasping at the top of the companionway.

"That's no way to approach the CO lad," the CPO snapped angrily. "Now make —"

"What is it?" Savage snapped as the men at the rum table turned to stare.

"*Mines,* sir ... scores of the buggers. Jerry must have laid 'em by night from the air. They're everywhere!"

Savage was no longer listening. Pushing the scared rating to one side and followed by the CPO like a faithful terrier, he mounted the steel stairs two at a time.

On the deck the master-at-arms was shouting angrily and passing out Lee Enfield rifles to the lookouts. Other young sailors, all obviously scared, were leaning over the rail to stare at the green water of the estuary. On the bridge his Number One had already reduced the destroyer's speed and she was responding. Savage nodded his approval. He dashed to the port side and took in the scene immediately.

"Old Jerry trick, sir," the CPO said. "Cheeky sods wait till the minesweepers clear the channel then they come in at night, drop their ruddy mines and hope that some poor bugger like us goes over one of 'em."

Savage nodded his head but he really wasn't listening. He was assessing the situation. His flotilla of four destroyers covered an area of perhaps a sea mile or so. To port and starboard there were other craft, too, a couple of gunboats, a tanker and a freighter. It seemed to him at that moment that not all of them were going out of this without a few bad bruises. They were all too close together in the narrow estuary. "But you, Savage," a hard little voice at the back of his mind rasped, "you can't afford to lose any craft or men now!"

He nodded his head as if in agreement and barked, "Master-at-arms."

"Sir?"

"Get some of your marksmen over here. I can see at least a dozen of the damned things here."

"Sir." The petty officer barked an order and two men doubled up to Savage, rifles at the ready.

Savage bit his bottom lip. He didn't dare explode the deadly devices too close to the ship. Any one of them could break the destroyer's back in an instant. So he said, "Fire at will. But not closer than a hundred yards to the ship."

The frightened young ratings needed no urging. They started firing immediately while Savage watched with bated breath and up above on the bridge his Number One steered the destroyer personally, sweat running down his face in streams.

The first mine was hit. Savage ducked instinctively as it went up in a great roar, followed an instant later by a huge fountain of whirling white water. "Good show," he bellowed above the racket. "Keep up the good work!"

He doubled up to the bridge. Even as he ran he knew that their luck wouldn't last forever. He clattered on the steel deck and took stock of the sea to the destroyer's front. It seemed empty of mines. The great steel balls of sudden death bobbing up and down in the sea with their lethal horns exposed seemed to be mostly to port and starboard. He made a snap decision. "Number One, give her full ahead!"

"What, sir," Number One replied aghast. "Our wash would drive those mines —"

"Full ahead I said," Savage interrupted him brutally.

"But the mines would then —" Again his words were drowned by the roar of an exploding mine and the cheers of the marksmen who had exploded it.

With a muffled curse Number One gave the required order. He knew, as did Savage, that the wash from their propellers might well push the mines in the direction of the two merchantmen to their rear, but he knew what Savage was thinking.

A moment later Savage expressed it aloud. "Number One, undoubtedly you think of me as the world's worst bastard. But my number one priority is my ships. Life at sea in wartime is bloody hard. It's every man for himself and I know where my duty lies."

Number One said nothing as the destroyer quivered and she gained speed. The deck tilted. At her stern the water turned from a dark sluggish green to a churning wild white as the speed of the props rose and rose. Speedily the mines started to be washed to the rear, heading straight for the two unsuspecting merchantmen.

Another mine exploded. Water shot to the sky. Now the destroyer was almost out of danger those mines which they had dodged rocking violently in their wake, were heading straight for the tanker. Number One said a quick silent prayer, the beads of sweat standing out on his forehead like opaque pearls. But his prayer was not answered.

Abruptly the tanker seemed to leap out of the water. An instant later there was a thick crump, a puff of deep black smoke and a great searing flame hissed the length of the tanker's long deck.

"Holy Christ!" The Number One groaned. "They've bought it the poor bastards!"

Savage grunted something and watched as the merchant sailors ran zigzagging down the length of the long deck, desperately trying to avoid the flames. Here and there they managed to do so, throwing themselves over the sides, choking and gasping as the icy water hit them and the flaming oil set off across the sea in an attempt to chase.

"Won't we heave to, sir?" the Number One cried in a shocked voice. "We're out of danger now. We can save a few of the poor sods."

Savage shook his head, his harsh face set and determined. "No we can't run that risk, Number One. We're out of the mines. We're not going back to chance running into one. Somebody else will pick them up in due course."

"But they won't last that long, sir," his Number One protested. "I think the flames —"

"*You* think nothing," Savage interrupted him brutally. "*I* do the thinking. Do you understand that," he spat out each word in a sudden fury. "The days of doing noble and gallant deeds are long over, Number One. This is total war, dog eat dog. No quarter given or expected." He swallowed hard and tried to contain his heaving chest. "We're fighting to survive and kill. Remember that, Number One, *survive and kill!* The rest of this is simply no-account ballast."

The first officer, shocked by Savage's action and the pure venom of his outburst, mumbled something and then concentrated on the business of conning the ship. Savage for his part stared grimly at the burning tanker, not even hearing the despairing cries of the survivors in the water. He had seen it all before. Undoubtedly he would see it again and then, with a bit of luck, he would die and that would be that.

Half an hour later the signal came through from the Admiralty. It was from Ian Fleming at Naval Intelligence. It read: *U-boat signalled position in clear. Stop. US Army Air Corps signals U-boat sunk. Stop. Identified as U-1226. Stop. Belongs to Wolf Pack Brandt. Stop. Indicates operation about to begin. Stop. Sail with all speed. Stop. Good hunting.*

Savage sat staring at the little piece of paper for a long time in his tiny cabin. The events of the day seemed to have blunted his emotions. He no longer felt the old excitement of the chase. To him, at that moment, with the dusk turning to night rapidly outside, it appeared simply that this was the natural order of things. The end to something. Finally he broke the heavy brooding silence of that tiny cabin, devoid of any personal memento, not even a photograph of his dead wife and children. He picked up the voice tube, whistled into it and commanded, "Number One, have the flotilla skippers report to me immediately. It's on!"

NINETEEN

"Stand by on the casement!" Brandt ordered, his voice echoing and re-echoing hollowly in the great submarine pen. *"Beide Motoren Steuer-bord voraus!"*

With a whine the motors started. The dirty, oily water of the pen was churned white as the screws began to turn and the first U-boat started to back out of the cover.

It was almost dawn. To the east the sky was beginning to flush a dirty white. By the time they entered the estuary and were on their way into the Atlantic Brandt knew it would be daylight. But it was a risk he was prepared to take.

By now he was quite sure the Tommies were aware of what was going on. They had sunk the sub carrying Schulze's Group so he was sure of it. All he could do was to attempt to catch them off balance. If he failed at least it would be daylight and his men would have a better chance of being rescued. If he succeeded then he would be in the wide, unbounded Atlantic and the Tommies would have a devil of a time trying to catch him.

The U-boat came out of the underground pen. In the old days there would have been a naval band playing them into the estuary with the French whores they had fucked the previous night waving their handkerchiefs dutifully and crying a few crocodile tears. But that had been in the days of victory when the U-boats had ruled the Atlantic. Now they stole out furtively, like thieves in the night, deadly afraid of being spotted.

Brandt flashed a look to his rear. The other boats of Wolf Pack Brandt were emerging from the pens. All was going to plan. He gave the estuary a quick look through his glasses: as he had always explained to his junior officers, "Be careful and methodical, then you survive. Be otherwise and you'll cure your throat ache for certain* but you'll make an early and beautiful corpse.'

There was nothing suspicious. He bent to the voice tube on the conning tower, "Both engines full ahead," he commanded and reaching for the pistol raised it and pulled the trigger.

As the lean grey craft quivered and trembled, a red Very flare exploded above his head and bathed his upturned face in an unreal glowing crimson. It was the signal he had agreed upon with the last remaining Luftwaffe fighter squadron in Lorient.

Now the three submarines formed an extended triangle as they moved into the estuary at ten knots. All had double watches posted and the gunners in their leather overalls were in position behind their guns, searching the dawn sky systematically, waiting for what had to come.

Brandt did the same, taking each quarter in turn, keen blue eyes tensed for that first dark moving speck which would mean trouble. Every now and again he would drop his gaze to the water in search of mines. But it was empty. The ancient wooden minesweeper which had gone out under the cover of darkness had, it seemed, done its job well. There were no mines.

But when the expected attack came it caught Brandt off guard. They had been sailing for quarter of an hour when there was a banshee-like screech followed an instant later by a tremendous explosion only metres away from his boat, sending it reeling and shuddering with the impact. On the deck one of the lookouts yelped with pain and clutched his hand to his shoulder, the blood jetting out of it in a red arc.

"Holy strawsack!" Brandt cursed. He had forgotten all about the Americans besieging Lorient. They had brought up long-range artillery. Now they were shelling the estuary from their positions miles away. "Damn ... damn!" he cried, as another huge shell came hurtling out of the sky. Was the shelling going to force him to dive

---

* The Knight's Cross of the Iron Cross was worn round the neck; hence to "cure your throat ache" meant winning that medal for valour.

before he intended? If so his whole strategy for getting out into the Atlantic safely might be placed in jeopardy.

But just as surprisingly as it had started the shelling ceased, leaving behind a loud echoing silence. Not for long. From the west there came the sound of aircraft engines. Brandt flung up his glasses. Dark shapes cut their way into the gleaming, calibrated circles of glass. "Beaufighters," he said the word to himself. "English Beaufighters."

The Americans and the British had coordinated their attacks obviously. As soon as the planes came in sight the American shelling ceased, just in case.

Brandt grinned softly. Excellent. So far everything was working out well.

Now the two-engined fighter-bombers came zipping in barely at mast-height, their props churning up the water, lashing it into a wild white fury. Brandt knew instinctively why they were coming in so low. They were carrying torpedoes. They had to come down that low in order to launch their deadly tin fish successfully.

He flung a look around his flotilla. The gunners were at their posts everywhere but all had obeyed his order not to fire. He nodded his approval. The Beaufighters were walking straight into the trap he had prepared for them.

The leading plane staggered. Something flashed beneath its stubby wings. There was a white splash of water. "She's launched her torpedo," a lookout cried as the plane soared high into the dawn sky, its pilot probably wondering why he had not yet been fired on.

"Hard to port," Brandt yelled urgently as he spotted the torpedo, trailing white bubbles behind it, heading straight for his boat. The helmsman reacted immediately. The U-boat shuddered as the helmsman flung the boat to one side. An instant later the torpedo hissed by them harmlessly.

Now more and more of the Beaufighters were falling out of the sky preparing to launch their torpedoes. Brandt flung an anxious look to the east. They'd be running out of luck soon, he knew that. One of the torpedoes would strike home.

Another torpedo knifed through the water heading for his boat. He made a split second decision and hoped it was the right one. He would not order a change of course. It was the right decision. If he had broken to port or starboard the tin fish would have struck the boat. Now it rushed by the U-boat harmlessly to explode on the far bank of the estuary a couple of seconds later.

"Now where the hell are the planes?" he asked himself angrily as one of the young gunners on the U-boat nearest him lost his nerve and began firing his twin spandaus at the attackers. Tracer streamed into the sky at a thousand rounds a minute. One of the Beaufighters staggered as if it had just run into an invisible wall. Smoke started to pour from its starboard engine. Desperately the pilot tried to keep his plane in the air. To no avail. Suddenly he lost control altogether. The Beaufighter smacked into the water nose first and went right under. A moment later the spluttering gasping survivors bobbed up in the water waving their hands and shouting for help.

Brandt frowned. It would be a long time before a boat would venture from the shore to help them and he was not going to stop now. They'd have to look after themselves, he told himself grimly.

Still the other Beaufighters kept attacking. They had regrouped, after the plane had been shot down. Now they came in skimming the waves, spaced out in an extended line, cannon chattering to put off any would-be gunner trying to attack from the stern so that the U-boats below presented a bigger target.

It was thus, racing in at three hundred miles an hour intent on their kills, that the Black Knights of Lorient, as the one remaining squadron of the Luftwaffe in the besieged port was known, caught the British completely by surprise.

Using their last reserves of fuel and ammunition the Me 109s fell on the attackers like angry black hawks, cannon and machineguns chattering furiously. The Beaufighters didn't stand a chance. In the first minute of action two were blown right out of the sky, exploding in mid-air, scattering metal everywhere in a gleaming hail of fragments. A third dropped its torpedo without aiming in a desperate attempt to gain speed. It roared over the far side of the estuary frantically attempting to shake off the following Me 109. But the German pilot didn't allow himself to be shaken off. He held on doggedly following every trick and turn the British pilot attempted until he as finally in range. His cannon chattered. Bits flew off the Beaufighter. Smoke started to stream from both engines. The canopy was flung open. Two black figures flung themselves into space. Moments later they were floating down by parachute as the Me 109 pilot rolled his plane joyously all over the dawn sky to celebrate his victory. Minutes later the remaining two enemy planes were shot down and the little battle was over.

"All right, Number One," Brandt was well satisfied with the way things had gone. "You can clear the decks for diving now. The Tommies have shot their bolt. They won't be able to mount another before we're out in the Atlantic."

"Ay ay, sir," Number One said smartly and pressed the button of the klaxon.

The siren shrilled its urgent warning. Men came running up from the deck. They squeezed past Brandt and went sliding down the rails on both sides of the conning tower leading into the U-boat's interior.

Brandt waited still they were all through. He took one long last look at the land to their stern then he, too, was clambering down the steps. They were on their way.

FOUR

TARGET NEW YORK

TWENTY

A high silver moon hung over the banks of drifting fog. In the spectral light the fog looked even thicker than it was. Not that Brandt minded. The fog was not thick enough to be dangerous but it did cover them as they recharged their batteries on the surface, a most dangerous operation at the best of times.

They had been sailing due west for two days now, travelling for much of the daylight hours underwater, maintaining visual contact with the other boats of the flotilla. For Brandt had imposed the strictest of radio silences. Now they were well past the Azores and the American planes based there. Still, he didn't allow his skippers to communicate with him save by signal lamp or flags.

Brandt watched the crew go about their business on the damp dripping deck, catching some fresh air after the stifling fetid odour down below, his hand cupped the glowing end of his cigar, his mind busy with a thousand and one problems

"Nigger sweat, sir?" He turned a little startled. It was Moses, as cooks were always called in the submarine service. He was holding a steaming hot coffee mug which smelled as if it had been well laced with spirits. "Dawn gunfire, sir," Moses added.

Brandt laughed softly and said, "Thanks. Keeping up naval tradition, eh, Moses?" At dawn in the submarine service the officer of the watch always had his "dawn gunfire", coffee laced with some kind of alcohol, served by the boat's Moses.

"Try to, sir," Moses answered dutifully. "I'd like to go regular after the war, but not as the Moses. Torpedo mate, something like that, sir."

"We'll see what we can do for you, Moses," Brandt said. "All right, you can go down below again."

"Thank you, sir. Ay, ay sir." The little cook disappeared into the interior once more and it struck Brandt anew that young volunteers for the U-boat arm, like Moses, really didn't know the danger they ran while on active service. Fifty percent of the submariners had not come back from combat patrols since 1939. One in two had died in action. Would the young Moses be one of them?

The thought turned his mind to the main problem: how to get into position off New York, fire the missiles and be gone before the Ami attack planes could scramble? In one way his problem had been eased a little by the sinking of the submarine carrying the Schulze Group. Now he wouldn't have to wait for their signals targeting their objective. He would simply fire blind and hope for the best, so that would cut down the time the Brandt Wolf Pack would have to remain on the surface. But there was still that nagging problem of the shallows just off the American coast and the close proximity of the Army Air Corps fields around New York City. Every minute would count if they were going to get in and out safely.

Thoughtfully Brandt sipped the hot mixture as the U-boat drifted through the mist like a grey ghost. Men were going about their duties, talking in whispers as if they might be heard. At the stern a rating was melting some ice which had formed during the night with a steam hose. Next to him Number One was making some rapid calculations, talking to himself as he did so. Automatically Brandt told himself that Number One had been at sea on active service for too long. It was always a bad sign when a man started to talk to himself.

Then, abruptly, with the clarity of a sudden vision Brandt had his solution. "In three devils' name, why didn't I think of that before?"

His Number One looked up startled. "Think of what, sir?" he asked.

By way of an answer Brandt drained the rest of his drink, coughed throatily and said, unable to conceal his excitement, "Come on. Down below. I want to look at the charts."

A minute later they were below, nostrils wrinkled in disgust as they smelled that old fetid stink, a compound of sweat, diesel, stale food and human gases. "Hand me the chart of the American East Coast, Number One, please."

Hurriedly the younger officer did as he was commanded and placed the big chart on the desk in front of Brandt. For a few moments Brandt stared at it in silence, his brow creased, harshly handsome face very thoughtful. Finally he spoke. "You know the problem, Number One? How to get in to New York, attack and be out before the Ami planes can be alerted. Time would be of the essence." His Number One nodded but said nothing. "I'd already decided to position the flotilla at Sandy Hook, here on the coast of New Jersey. Even without Schulze's men targeting for us I think we have a good chance of hitting something important from there to the east rather than further north."

"Yessir, I see," the other officer replied dutifully, though really he didn't.

"All the same you know the range of those missiles, so we'd have to go within thirty miles of the American coast." He did a quick calculation from kilometres to sea miles. "My guess is," he said after a moment's thought, "that the Ami pilots would be alerted and scrambled within ten to fifteen minutes of the first missile striking home."

"They weren't very quick at Pearl Harbor when the little yellow men attacked them," Number One objected.

"That was back in 1941. The Amis have learned a lot about war since. So let us be realistic. Scrambled within a quarter of hour the planes would probably be able to cover those thirty sea miles to our original firing site within ten minutes. So we've got a quarter of an hour to get out to sea again once we've fired our six missiles." He shrugged. "That timescale doesn't give us much of a chance of escaping does it, Number One?"

"I suppose not, sir," he agreed hesitantly. "But I'm sure we can do it. It's a risk that we will have to take for Folk, Fatherland and Fuhrer," he added proudly.

Brandt knew that unlike most professional naval officers his Number One was a keen Nazi, but he didn't chide him on that score. Instead he said simply, "Tell that to the loved ones of these boys all around us if we don't get them back to *Folk, Fatherland and Fuhrer,"* he emphasised the words a little cynically, "in safety. No, Number One, we must come up with something else."

"What, sir?"

"A decoy."

"A decoy?" the other man echoed in bewilderment.

"Yes. Here at Cape Cod in their state of Massachusetts."

"But there's nothing of any importance there, sir," the Number One objected.

"I know. I sailed those waters back in '42. We made a killing. We sank 400,000 tons of American shipping that winter, more than was sunk at Pearl Harbor. The Amis were terribly slack. They had no blackout and you could easily see the ships coming out from Boston. Why," he chuckled softly at the memory, "they even had Chatham Lighthouse here flashing a beam every ten seconds to guide us in so to speak." His tone changed. "Now, this is the way I see it, one of the flotilla will fire its missiles at extreme range at the Cape Cod area. Even if they only hit the beach or a holiday bungalow, no matter. The hits will be recorded and the air force scrambled. The whole of that area will be alerted as happened in Oregon when the Japs dropped their fire bombs by balloon in '43. All will be confusion, believe you me. But attention will be focused on that area while we sneak up Sandy Hook and fire our missiles and, hopefully, in the general chaos escape without notice."

The younger officer's face lit up at the idea. "Excellent idea! That should work all right. But there's one defect, sir."

"What's that?"

"We shall be wasting six valuable missiles. I mean, sir, we haven't come all this way not to make every missile count." The Number One's face twisted bitterly, "And make those Jewish air gangsters pay for what they have done to our cities over the last years."

"Twelve missiles landing in the New York City area will be quite sufficient to bring the war home to those Jewish 'air gangsters' as you call them. Thereafter my prime consideration is my boys." He swept the interior with a swing of his arm. "Now make a visual to the other skippers. I want them aboard as soon as possible for an instant conference. I'll brief them and then we'll select the skipper who's going to make the great attack on Chatham Beach."

Half an hour later the four skippers had almost finished their little conference with the crew of Brandt's boat standing respectfully in the background, straining to hear what was being said. "Well, gentlemen, now the time has come to pick the one among you who will play the decoy, and I can assure you that role is just as important as the attack on New York itself. Number One, the cards."

His Number One placed a greasy pack of cards used by the petty officers to play Skat during their off-duty watches on the little metal table.

"I have to take overall responsibility so I can't be the decoy," Brandt explained. "So it's up to you."

He looked at them for a moment in the glowing green light: Witt, a former petty officer who had come up through the ranks and who was a bit of a bully; Baeder, tough, four-square, a skipper who had been a mate on a freighter before the war; and the youngest, Blau*, 'blue by name, blue by nature' as his crew joked about him behind his skinny back, nervous and a bit pedantic. He looked exactly what he had been before the war, a music teacher in a girls' school.

"All right," Brandt said. "High card loses. High card becomes the decoy."

Witt didn't hesitate. He grabbed a card with his hairy paw and guffawed when he saw what it was. "Can't get any lower than that, can yer?" It was the two of clubs.

Then it was Baeder's turn. Silently he turned his card over. It was the seven of hearts.

Now all attention turned to Blau. The skinny officer licked his thin lips as he always did when he prepared to play his flute during his off-duty time. Gingerly he reached out to pick his card. His hand hovered above the pack.

"Come on," Brandt urged. "We haven't got all day. The fog's clearing."

Blau selected his card. He turned it over reluctantly. Perhaps he already guessed he was going lose the draw. He did. His card was the queen of diamonds.

Witt guffawed and Baeder said, "Hard luck, Blau."

144

"As I said, the decoy is just as important as the actual assault, gentlemen," Brandt said hurriedly, seeing the look on Blau's face. "All right, last words. Today is Tuesday 12 December. We shall continue on this course 'till Thursday 14. I shall give you a visual, Blau, and then you'll make your own course to any point of your choice off Cape Cod. Keep as far out as possible. Ensure only that when the attack is made, your missiles hit the beach and set off the alarm. *Klar?"*

"Klar."

"Now, gentlemen," Brandt was unusually solemn, for him. "I shall tell you the great secret. Our forces all along the Western Front attack at five hundred hours on the morning of Saturday 16 December. We shall do our best to coordinate our attack with that in Europe. Blau, you shall commence your attack at five hundred hours and then get out as if the Devil himself were after you. Our attack on New York will then commence at five thirty. Now, there is no more to be said".

Awkwardly his officers clicked to attention in the confined space of the sub's interior. Brandt returned their salute. Then they were gone, clattering up the conning tower, each man wrapped in a cocoon of his own thoughts.

Brandt watched them go in silence. Finally he turned to the Number One and said almost defiantly, "Well, there you are, Number One, that's the way it's going to be. Please brief the crew." Then he bent his head over the charts. There was a lot to be done.

TWENTY-ONE

"This is the captain," Savage's voice echoed metallically over the loudspeakers up and down the mist-shrouded decks, through the narrow companionways, into the messrooms and offices. "I shall now tell you the purpose of our mission."

Everywhere the men, darning socks, peeling potatoes, drinking their cocoa or rolling "ticklers" from packets of loose tobacco stopped what they were doing. Eagerly they cocked their heads in the direction of the nearest tannoy.

"We are to apprehend and stop one flotilla, the Brandt Wolf Pack, of Jerry U-boats from attacking New York."

Men whistled from narrowed lips. Others looked at their "oppos" in disbelief. A man eating a banger off a tin plate of gravy dropped it in his surprise and splashed himself with the thick goo. He didn't even notice. "Cor, ferk a duck," Wide Boy, the ship's cockney spiv said in amazement. "Would get believe it. The squareheads are going to duff up New York and yours truly is gonna stop 'em. Cor, ferk a duck!"

"We know this Brandt Wolf Pack has already sailed from Lorient. An attempt was made to stop them there but failed. Now they are somewhere in Mid-Atlantic and so far they haven't broken radio silence so we can't locate them. We think that presently they're somewhere in the black hole."

"What's that when it's at 'ome?" Wide Boy asked Chippy, the ship's carpenter, who was a grizzled old three striper.

"Where's you bin since yer was welped?" the carpenter asked scornfully. "Some of you young sprogs don't know nuthin!

It's the bit in the Atlantic too far from patrols by air from either our side or the Yanks' side to reach. That's yer 'ole."

"However, we are confident that the Boche will break radio silence sooner or later," Savage went on. "They've already done it once in this bad business and we consequently nailed the Jerry sub in question. We feel they'll do it again."

The young sailors looked at each other impressed and even the old hands looked a little proud, as if they were somehow personally responsible for having sunk the enemy craft.

"Now, I am asking all you deck men," Savage went on, "to keep a special lookout. You radiomen, too. Be on your toes all the time. If the Jerries don't break radio silence, which I think they will, they *will* have to surface to recharge their batteries. We're in for a spell of very cold weather the weather man has told me. There'll be no snow so that means once we've passed the hole and close up to the American seaboard visibility will be excellent. The lookouts will be able to see for miles. All right, men, that's all, but keep on yer toes." The tannoy system went dead and slowly the men went back to their duties or their other activities, pondering the captain's words, many of them realising for the first time since they had left harbour that this was the real thing; that they were now engaged in a cruel cat-and-mouse game which would have a lethal outcome. As a suddenly chastened Wide Boy expressed it to the Chippy, "Christ, we're gonna see some action."

To which the latter replied scornfully, "What d' yer think, frigging pints of beer and 'am sandwiches?"

Now the cold was intense. Under a hard blue sky the wind came down straight from the Arctic Circle. Within hours the destroyer's superstructure and deck turned a harsh brilliant white and the ratings were kept busy hosing down the guns and essential fittings with steam hoses to disperse the hoar frost.

Those standing watch, huddled as they were in duffel coats and as many layers of sweaters as they could find, felt the deadly chill creep slowly upwards from feet to thigh, from thigh to shoulders, reaching icily for the face. Every few minutes they wiped the tears from their eyes to prevent their eyelashes from freezing up and rubbed their ears and noses. All prayed that they would be relieved soon and allowed to return to the warm fug below deck, though even there their torture wouldn't end. For the agony of returning circulation that came with the warmth was almost as bad to bear.

But as Captain Savage had predicted visibility was absolutely perfect. Sweeping forward in an extended line, each destroyer covering a grid of twenty miles, advancing ever westwards, the lookouts could see for miles.

Savage seemed to live on the bridge. Tirelessly he swept his binoculars along the horizon, ignoring the freezing wind, searching with almost fanatical energy for the craft they had come to destroy.

More than once his Number One, the only officer aboard apart from the flotilla surgeon who knew just how sick the skipper was, chided him with an urgent, "You mustn't overdo it, sir. You must rest more in your cabin, sir. There are lookouts enough."

But Savage wouldn't be deterred. "Stop playing nanny, Number One," he would snap not taking his gaze off the horizon for a moment, "I'm all right."

But despite all their efforts the horizon remained stubbornly empty. It was as if they were all alone in this harsh white heaving world. It was the same down below where the radio operators hunched over their detectors and radio, twirling the bands, adjusting their earphones all the time. The airwaves remained empty of any radio traffic that had originated from the enemy submarines. Twice they picked up coded signals from Kiel and Berlin which they knew were intended for the U-boats — though they would have to wait for the Admiralty decodes from London before they knew what the messages contained. But in both cases there were no replies.

"He's a tough, cunning bugger, that Kapitanleutnant Brandt," Savage explained as he sat with his Number One in the wardroom before dinner, sipping a pink gin. "He's their last ace, the best of the lot in my opinion. I'm beginning to think he won't break radio silence until after he's carried out his attack, though naturally we're not going to allow him to get that far."

He gave a tired smile and Number One told himself once again the skipper looked very sick with those deep circles under his eyes and the lines etched around his mouth.

"Yes, my feeling is, Number One, that we're only going to catch Brandt if one of his subordinates makes a mistake."

"How do you mean, sir?"

"Well, surfaces at the wrong time ... or has a radio operator practising in his spare time with the power on by mistake ... dumping garbage which isn't weighed down so that it remains on the surface. There are umpteen things which have happened in the past to give away a sub."

Number One nodded his understanding. If Brandt was an ace U-boat commander then Savage was an ace destroyer skipper. He knew all the tricks. If anyone was going to scupper the Boche it would be Captain Savage.

On the second day after they had passed the "hole" they sighted a large fast motor vessel on the horizon, a white bone in its teeth, going at a fast lick. Next to the Captain on the bridge the Number One hurriedly focused his glasses and made her out. "She's neutral, sir. Argentinean, the *Reina del Mar*. I remember from the identification tables. She's a fast liner. The Americans have been using her for the last year or so to bring their beef to Britain."

Savage lowered his glasses. "Do you think the Boche know that, about the beef?"

"I suppose so, sir."

"Then she's not really neutral, is she. She'd be a legitimate target for any German sub, eh?"

The Number One looked at Savage worried. "You wouldn't, would you?" he stammered.

"I would." We're going to ask her to heave to while we examine the ship's manifest and ask for information. The Boche might just rise to the bait. A blockade breaker and a British destroyer. A juicy twenty thousand odd tons to report back to Kiel, what!"

Now Number One really looked shocked. "But the risk —"

"It's a risk we've got to take, Number One," he cut his protest off brutally. "Now, prepare to signal her to heave to and have a boarding party standing by."

"Ay, ay, sir," Number One said miserably and left, telling himself that this day Savage was really living up to his bloody name.

Savage crossed with the boarding party himself. It looked better to have a full captain dealing with the liner's skipper. He didn't like South Americans; he had had dealings enough with them on cruises "showing the flag" before the war. The British-Argentineans were all right for the most part, but the rest of the country's upper class had been patently fascist. For most of the war they had sided with Hitler. Now Germany was losing they were trying to improve their relationships with Britain by shipping much needed beef to the UK.

The liner's captain was barely polite. He gave Savage a cold salute and said in fair English, "We are a friendly neutral taking supplies to your country. Why stop us?"

"Ship's manifest, sir," Savage answered just as coolly, "And have you any information?"

"About submarines? No. But I do realise that the longer we are stopped like this the greater our danger from submarines."

"I understand that. Let us make our examination as quick as possible, then."

In the event Savage drew out the examination of the manifest with its details of crew and cargo as long as possible, asking what he knew were idiotic questions, praying that they had been sighted by one of Brandt's Wolf Pack. Next to him the captain glowered and muttered angrily under his breath in Spanish, occasionally going to the porthole to look out as if he half expected to see a U-boat out there.

In the end Savage said, "All looks very much in order, captain."

"Hombre, es todo claro!" he snapped and then in English said, "Can I get underway now?" He was angry; he didn't offer Savage the customary parting drink.

"Of course, just collect my party." Savage saluted and strolled casually onto the deck where the petty officer in charge, all helmet, cutlass and white gaiters, bellowed, "Boarding party close up now!"

The sailors sprang to attention woodenly to the jeers and catcalls of the *Reina del Mar's* crew. Moments later they were on their way back to the destroyer while high above them the engine-room telegraphs began to clatter and the big ex-liner started to draw away.

Savage's Number One was waiting for him as he clattered up the steel ladder. "Sir ... sir," he yelled excitedly above the roar of the *Reina del Mar's* powerful engines.

Savage cocked his head to one side. "What is it, Number One?"

"Sparks ... Sparks has just picked up a signal. It's not very strong and of course we don't know what it means. But it's high speed morse."

"Boche?"

"Exactly, sir, and it's on the U-boat channel."

Savage laughed out loud with sheer delight. "They've fallen for it," he gasped as he clambered over the rail.

"Looks very like it, sir."

Savage thought a moment. "Signal the others. Just the code word *alert*. And, Number One, it all depends on how quickly we hear from Bletchley."

"Right away, sir," Number One exclaimed now carried away by sudden excitement. He doubled to the radio cabin while Savage leaned a little wearily against the rail, the icy wind forgotten, a sudden throbbing in his chest. He grimaced, aware again abruptly that his time was limited.

For a moment he shook his head like a boxer trying to overcome a nasty punch which was threatening to knock him out. Again he felt that icy wind straight from the Arctic. He was still alive, wasn't he, he demanded. He could still move, think and act. "Of course you can, dammit man!" a harsh little voice at the back his mind rasped. "Stop feeling sorry, man. Get on with the job. Collar that Boche bastard, Brandt before you snuff it and you can die happy. Now move!"

Two hours later the signal came from the Admiralty. Breathing a little faster, Savage waited in the tiny radio cabin as Sparks scribbled down the groups of coded figures and Number One began decoding them straight away. *Signal ... U-1223 ... Request permission to sink neutral vessel Reina del Mar ... carrying food to UK ... Recorded position ... latitude ...*

"We've got them, Number One!" Savage exclaimed triumphantly. "The U-1200s are Brandt's Wolf Pack. Praise the Lord, we've got them! Now come on. Let's get to the chart room in

151

double quick time." Like two excited schoolboys the officers ran out of the radio cabin leaving Sparks to scratch the back of his head and mutter, "Christ Almighty, officers an 'gents ... officers and gents!"

TWENTY-TWO

"That arsehole Witt!" Brandt raged as he read the signal for a second time, his gaze full of disbelief. "Compromises the whole mission so that he could cure his throatache by sinking the *Reina del Mar!* Heaven, arse and cloudburst, the swine ought to be court martialed for this!" Unable to contain his anger any longer Brandt crumpled up the signal and threw the paper violently at the bulkhead.

"At least Kiel didn't give him permission, sir," his Number One tried to appease a furious, red-faced Brandt.

"I should damn well hope not! All the months of planning and plotting that have gone into this mission and that bullying bastard has virtually thrown it away for his own shitting personal glory!"

The younger officer said, "I'm sure the enemy is in no position to crack the Enigma, sir. We've been using it since '39 and it has never been compromised."

"I know ... I know," Brandt retorted hotly. "That's not the point. Their detectors will have pin-pointed a submarine in this part of the Atlantic. Now do you suppose they'll be sitting on their fat arses twiddling their thumbs and smoking their frigging pipes? Of course they won't! They will have already alerted their surface craft to come looking for us. Their recce planes will be out, too. *Mensch, das ist doch zum Kotzen!*" He slammed his fist against the casing.

The duty watch kept their eyes lowered as the skipper raged at the top of his voice. They had never seen Kapitanleutnant Brandt in such a temper. So, they concluded, whatever had happened was serious, very serious indeed.

With an effort of sheer, naked willpower Brandt controlled himself. "All right," he said suddenly, his voice normal once more, the crimson draining from his thin unshaven cheeks. "What are we going to do about it?"

"We can assume that either they have surface craft in the area or if not they'll have dispatched them from Halifax, Norfolk and the like, sir. And that will take time."

"Exactly, Number One. If the second case is correct we'll be all right, I feel. We shall be well away from this area by then. But we can't bank on it unfortunately." He thought for a moment while the other officer waited tensely.

Finally Brandt made his decision. "We shall now run on the surface at full speed. At seventeen knots full out we could be well out of this area, given, say, three or four hours grace." He shrugged. "Hopefully! Double watches will be posted Again all signals will be visual." Then as afterthought he added, "Blau can set course for Cape Cod immediately. That just leaves the three of us in visual contact and that's a big enough target as it is. But it can't be helped. All right, Number One, take her."

"Jawohl, Kommandant! Number One snapped promptly. He pressed the klaxon. The siren shrilled. The on-duty watch prepared to raise the boat. Compressed air and water rushed from the tanks as the Number One eyed the gauges keenly, knowing he must keep the sub on an even trim. "Stop at ten metres," he ordered.

The U-boat remained suspended just below the surface of the water as he commanded, "Up periscope!"

There was a slither of polished greased metal and the periscope slid up the tube. Hurriedly the Number One pushed his battered cap brim to the back of his head and peered through the instrument, swinging it round carefully through a 360 degree arc, using the intensifier to search the far horizon. "Nothing," he said over his shoulder for the captain's benefit.

"Good," Brandt snapped.

"Take her up!" the Number One commanded as the deck crew struggled into their thick leather overalls, fur hats and sou'westers.

Moments later the U-boat broke the surface. Her hatches were open. The fans whirred. Icy cold air streamed into the interior to be sucked up greedily by the men constantly nauseated by the fug inside.

Number One clattered up the dripping rungs followed by Brandt and the gun crew, plus the lookouts, huge binoculars slung round their necks.

Swiftly the gun crew and the flak gunners manned their weapons while Brandt scanned the horizon hurriedly. But it was empty, just the hard blue sea, its surface whipped up into white ice devils by the freezing wind coming from the Arctic. "So far so good," he muttered to himself. He did a 360 degree survey of the sky but it was empty, too. Not an aircraft in sight.

Now he waited till the other three U-boats surfaced. They had been sailing at periscope depth at Brandt's orders. They would have seen his boat surface. They would do the same. He bent and called into the interior, "Signaller up here, at the double!"

Witt's boat was the first to surface some three hundred metres to port. Brandt's face hardened. He turned to the signaller and ordered, "Send this." The signaller bent over his lamp. "Consider yourself under open arrest for insubordination. I shall institute court martial proceedings against you when we return to the Reich." *If* a harsh little voice at the back of his mind sneered. Brandt ignored it. "Remain on the surface now. Continue on this course at top speed."

Witt's signaller acknowledged but Witt made no reference to the business of open arrest. Brandt knew he would be fuming. He would see his chances of becoming a regular naval officer, his dream since he had joined the Kriegsmarine, going out of the window.

Then as the other boats started to surface Brandt repeated his orders, first to Baeder and then to Blau.

Baeder's signaller acknowledged with a simple, "Understood", but Blau obviously seemed unhappy with the new turn of events for he signalled: "If mission compromised suggest request HQ for alternative or cancellation."

Brandt laughed grimly and his Number One said: "Blau's beginning to shit himself." His voice was full of contempt. Next to them the signaller pretended to be examining his lamp. It wasn't wise to know what officers thought of each other, especially these days. But he'd have something to whisper to the others in his mess this evening. Bully Boy Witt under open arrest and Blau getting the wind up. Thank God they had Brandt for a skipper!

"Yes," Brandt agreed as he thought over Blau's request for a moment, "the worm's there all right. But we can do nothing about it, *yet*. Signaller."

"Sir?"

"Signal U-1226. Orders will be carried out as originally planned."

Hastily the signaller began to work his lamp, clanking the shutter up and down on the harsh white light that came from it.

A moment later the reply, "Understood. But I wish it recorded that I sail under duress."

"Damn the man's impudence!" Brandt snapped, face grim and set. "Signaller. Send this. "Leave at once. No more talk. End!"

He turned to his Number One. "I don't know, but the future doesn't look too rosy for Wolf Pack Brandt, does it? One skipper under open arrest, the other filling his pants and ready to disobey orders."

The Number One frowned but said nothing.

An hour later Blau's boat had virtually disappeared, heading north-west at top speed. The rest now sailed in formation with a distance of some five hundred metres between each U-boat. Nerves were tense. Now the young submariners knew that there had been a serious disagreement between their officers and that the Pack's position had become known. They knew, too, that the closer they came to the American coast the more likely they could expect trouble from the many US airfields which lined the shores of New England, and Virginia.

Brandt was aware of the mood of his young sailors. On his boat he was here there and everywhere, encouraging those who were on watch, up and below deck, chatting and cracking jokes with those who were off watch. He called Moses to his tiny box of a cabin and told him, "Moses, pull something out of the hat for the main meal. Give them something special and a ration of a bottle of beer per man. And no peasoup," he warned. "They fart enough in this place as it is. The methane level in my boat must be the highest in the whole of the U-boat arm."

Moses grinned and said, "Don't worry, sir there'll no fart soup this day." Then he was off to carry out the skipper's orders.

By late afternoon, with the sun a pale yellow ball on the horizon to the west, they were well away from where Witt had betrayed their position and Brandt felt a little reassured for there had been no sign of the enemy. In an hour the sun would be below the horizon and then they were out of danger, especially from the air. He began to relax a little telling himself that things would be all right after all. Another forty eight hours and it would be over.

By that time he was back on the conning tower, watching as the lookouts searched the horizon for anything that might spell danger. But the horizon remained empty save for a few small black clouds which, with the rising temperatures, indicated that they might have snow soon. He nodded his approval. A snowstorm would help provide cover, too, until darkness fell.

"It looks as if we're going to get away with it, sir," his Number One confirmed his own feeling as Moses came up bringing them mugs of steaming hot coffee.

"Real *bean* coffee, too, gentlemen," he said handing them the mugs. "I'm going to feed them goulash and noodles, together with a helping of —" He stopped short suddenly in mid-sentence, mouth gaping foolishly.

Brandt looked at the little cook. "What is it, Moses?" he demanded. "Watch that mug, man you're going to drop it!"

Next moment Moses did so. It clattered to the deck scattering black coffee everywhere as Moses yelled, "Astern, sir! Am I seeing right, sir?"

Brandt and the Number One swung round. To the east it was almost dusk, but there was enough light to see four dark shapes steaming towards them. As one they threw up their glasses and adjusted the sights. "Tribal class, Tommy destroyers," Number One announced immediately . "Couldn't mistake 'em!"

"Agreed. They're on to us. "All right, clear the deck." He pressed the button of the klaxon. Its shrill warning shrieked throughout the boat.

The men knew what to do without orders. Hurriedly, but controlled, the crew clattered into the conning tower and slid to the bottom one by one while Brandt waited impatiently, knowing that the English destroyers were going twice his speed. Anxiously he flashed a look to left and right. Witt and Baeder had spotted the enemy ships, too. They were beginning to submerge as well, a furious white swell at the boats' bows as they started to go down.

In a matter of moments the deck was cleared. Brandt waited no longer. He slipped through the hatch. With his one hand he secured and dropped to the bottom of the conning tower where the deck was wet with seawater. "Prepare for silent running!" he commanded as the green lighting changed to an eerie, unreal, glowing red.

Moses, still holding the one remaining mug of coffee, shook his head and muttered, "Let's thank God for what we're now going to receive, and it won't be frigging goulash!"

TWENTY-THREE

"Meine Herren, der Fuhrer!" the giant SS adjutant bellowed at the top of his voice.

Hurriedly the Prominenz, field marshals, generals, admirals, SS Obergruppenfuhrer and a few civilians sprang to attention. Skorzeny and Doenitz in the front rank threw up their right arms stiffly and yelled, "Heil Hitler!" The Wehrmacht generals, most of whom had lost friends and comrades in an wholesale slaughter of Army generals after the failed assassination of the Fuhrer, were more circumspect. They merely raised their hands to their caps in the traditional military salute.

An old man crawled in. His face was grey and hollow, his hands trembled violently. He dragged one leg behind him. With the help of the giant adjutant the man who ruled Germany's destiny was guided slowly to the huge table where he collapsed gratefully in the proffered chair and tried to hide his trembling hands beneath it.

"Meine Herren," the adjutant bellowed as if he were on the parade ground, *"nehmen Sie Platz!"*

There was a hurried shuffling of feet, a scrapping of chairs and the Prominenz took their seats under the watchful eyes of the SS guards who lined the walls, each man a giant with a submachinegun slung across his chest. They waited, the only sound the Fuhrer's heavy laboured breathing.

Finally he began to speak. At first he was slow and hesitant, but as the colour started to flood back into his cheeks his voice grew stronger, more confident, faster. Fire came back to his eyes and he again wielded that same hypnotic power as of old, as he harangued the Prominenz. Germany had been forced to go to war in 1939 to protect itself, he told them. Since then Germany had had tremendous victories and some terrible defeats. Yet, right throughout the years of battle that lay behind them the German people had always shown toughness, stubbornness and daring. "Germany," he declared fervently, "has made it clear to the enemy that whatever he does he will never be able to count on the capitulation of the German people, never, never, never!" Spittle spat from his mouth as he uttered the words.

Now Germany was faced with fighting against a great coalition. But they were a strange mix, ultra capitalist states on the one hand, ultra-Marxist on the other. "Even the ultra capitalist states, Britain and America, are strange bedfellows. The English are dead set on retaining their decaying Empire, while the American capitalists under that Jew Roosevelt are equally dead set on taking over what is left of that Empire."

He paused, breathing hard as if he had just run a great race. Hurriedly an aide offered him a glass of water and he swallowed down a handful of the sixty-odd pills he took each day. Almost immediately the Fuhrer's eyes started to glow again and the heavy breathing ceased.

"Now, gentlemen," Hitler continued with renewed energy. "All of you in this room are privy to the great secret. You all know that in exactly thirty-six hours I shall launch a great attack on the Americans on the Western Front which will drive through their positions in the Belgian Ardennes. From there my brave panzers will cut through the enemy rear, cross the River Meuse and then head for the enemy's major supply port, Antwerp. It will be a great military victory." He raised a finger as if in warning. "But it will be a great political one, too. For it will split the British Army from the American one and Churchill is scraping the barrel. He has no more reserves. Neither has de Gaulle in France. So, what can the enemy do?" He shrugged expressively in the Austrian fashion. "If he's sensible he will reach a separate peace with us so that we can deal with the Russians without having to fight on two fronts."

He let his words sink in for a moment. Most of the Wehrmacht generals remained stony-faced and unimpressed. They thought the Fuhrer was living in a dream world. They believed that Antwerp as an objective was unrealistic. But they knew any objection to Hitler's plans these days was dangerous. Hadn't he recently strung up elderly Field Marshals with chicken wire and had a private film made of their death struggles?

But Hitler was still as observant as he had once been back in the heady days of victory in the early '40s. "I see my dear generals," the sneer was obvious, Hitler hated these generals whom he called privately "monocle Fritzes", "that I haven't altogether convinced you. England, you would probably say, *has* scraped the barrel as far as manpower and resources go but *not* America. America has still several divisions in England waiting to be sent to the continent and probably scores more in the USA. Ah!"

Again the Fuhrer raised a shaking finger as if in warning. "But my dear Skorzeny over there," he beamed at the scarfaced SS giant, "has taken measures to ensure that those reserves do not reach the battlefield and that America's morale will be shaken to such a degree that its people will literally beg its government to sue for peace."

He let his words sink in, making them wait, wondering what he had still got up his sleeve. It was an old orator's trick which he had used a hundred times or more before and he noted with satisfaction that "monocle Fritzes" fell for it as easily as a mass rally of working-class men.

"Why will they? I shall tell you. In thirty six hours over a quarter of a million fit young German men imprisoned in POW camps the length of the British isles will break out of their cages and march on London. More men than you have in your whole army, General von Manteuffel," he indicated the skinny diminutive commander of the Fifth Army which would lead the great attack. "A whole army in the midst of the enemy's camp, a real life Trojan Horse."

Now he could see he had them. The Prominenz looked startled, smiled suddenly, whispered happily among themselves with much nodding of heads and excited intakes of breath. Yes, he told himself, his statement had really gone home.

"But that is not all, gentlemen. Skorzeny there has yet another and even more startling trick up his sleeve." He beamed fondly at the other man. Skorzeny looked down modestly at his fingernails. "On this coming Saturday we shall not only attack in the

Ardennes and in England, we shall also attack New York, five thousand kilometres on the other side of the Atlantic!"

There was a gasp of surprise from the generals. They sat up startled. Hitler had known his words would have that effect. For that reason, he had picked the statement to be his last at this Thursday conference.

"V-2s fired from a flotilla of U-boats will begin landing on New York on Saturday morning just as they have been landing on London since September. But this time they will hit their targets precisely, guided by our own people who are now in New York itself." Doenitz flashed a look at Skorzeny. Skorzeny looked away. "Unlike the British who are, after all, a Germanic race and are basically stubborn and brave and do not panic easily, the New Yorkers are a mixture of a dozen different inferior races, mainly Hebrew. Undoubtedly they will panic outright and anyone who has the slightest knowledge of American politics knows just how easily and swiftly their presidents yield to public outcry and pressure. *Meine Herren,*" he stared around the room once again the proud supreme warlord, "by Christmas at the latest I am confident that the Anglo-Americans will have got rid of that old soak Churchill, perhaps even the Jew Roosevelt, and will be suing for peace. We shall have a great victory." He paused and then said, *"Meine Herren,* as you know I abhor alcohol, but on this one occasion I think I shall relent and take a glass of good German champagne with you, none of that French stuff." He clapped his hands.

As if they had been listening at the door a stream of white-jacketed mess stewards came hurrying in bearing gleaming silver trays, heavy with glasses. Hitler waited till each of the Prominenz was standing, holding a glass, then he said, his voice full of brimming confidence, "Gentlemen, to victory in 1944, and death to New York!"

"Victory in 1944," they cried as one, elbow held at a forty-five degree angle to the chest as military regulations prescribed. "And death to New York!"

"Ex!"

"Ex!" they drained their glasses in one gulp. As one they threw the empty glasses at the opposite wall where they shattered in a burst of flying glass.

The conference was over. They saluted and began to leave, talking excitedly among themselves, retrieving their pistols which had been taken off them by the SS guards, their briefcases and coats, heading for the waiting cars where the drivers were already gunning the engines, filling the icy December air with smoke as if impatient to be off.

Skorzeny got into the back seat of his Horch. But before he could leave for his new HQ on the German border Doenitz held up his hand, thin fanatical face set and hard, "We have heard nothing from Brandt save a message from that dolt Leutnant Witt twenty hours ago."

Skorzeny looked up at him through the open window. "Does that mean the enemy is on to Wolf Pack Brandt?"

"Not that I know of. We have been monitoring their signals with extreme care. So far they have made no reports of a sighting to their various headquarters."

Skorzeny breathed a sigh of relief. "Thank God for that!" he said.

Doenitz hesitated before he finally spoke, making every word count. "You saw the Fuhrer back there. That toast of his, 'death to New York' and all that. You must realise how dear this mission is to his heart, Skorzeny."

"I understand, Herr Grossadmiral."

"Then you must understand, too, that there can be no failure, absolutely none!" Doenitz continued directing that fierce chilling gaze of his on Skorzeny. "If there is heads will roll and I can assure you that it won't be mine. Goodbye."

"Goodbye," Skorzeny heard himself say, feeling an icy finger of fear tracing its way slowly down his spine. For a moment he sat there, mind totally blank, while the driver gunned the cold engine impatiently. All around the others were departing with sentries springing to attention and orderly officers clicking their heels to make bows from the waist. All was confident haste and Prussian military precision. But suddenly it no longer impressed Skorzeny.

"Driver, you may go," he ordered, a new plan beginning to form in his mind, a personal one. Whatever the outcome of the attack on New York, whether it failed or succeeded, he knew that the Amis would want their revenge. Already he was a marked man. They would brand him a major war criminal and he knew what his fate would be if the Amis ever caught him. He must make plans for the future. He must plan a new identity and a means of escape when the Third Reich fell apart, which he knew with the absolute certainty of a sudden vision, it would.

The staff car rolled past a column of young soldiers singing lustily, their honest young faces wreathed in the grey fog of their own breath. Suddenly he saw death in all their faces. They were the cannon fodder sent to the coming slaughter. "But not me," he whispered to himself. "Not me."

Thus, as the car rolled towards the new front and five thousand kilometres away Wolf Pack Brandt fought its last battle, Obersturmbannfuhrer Otto Skorzeny began to make his separate peace.

TWENTY-FOUR

"Ach du heilige Scheisse!" Witt cursed as the first depth charge exploded somewhere to port. "The Tommies are on to us!" Next instant the U-boat heeled wildly sending the crew grabbing rapidly for a hold.

"Stop both!" Witt yelled. "Rig for silent running!"

Startled as they were the young crewmen went through the routine with practised ease as the roar of the first pattern of depth charges died away to be followed almost instantly by that frightening "ping-ping" of the destroyer's instrument bouncing the echo off the submarine's outer casing.

Inside, in the eerie glowing red light, the crew waited in tense silent apprehension. There was something very awesome about that noise. Even the most unimaginative of them sensed it knowing that somewhere up above there was an enemy seeking them out ready to destroy them in an instant.

"Ship's propellers, sir," the operator at the hydrophone said quietly, his face as he listened intently to the sound lathered in sweat, as if it had been greased.

Witt swallowed hard. At the beginning of the war he had been a tough reliable petty officer with ambitions and he had been brave as long as he had good skipper who gave the orders. Now his nerve was long gone. Already, although the cat-and-mouse game had not really started yet, his heart was beating like a trip-hammer and his big paws were beginning to shake.

"Closing in, sir," the hydrophone operator called out softly, at the same time making an adjustment to his instrument.

Ping ... ping ... ping ... ping, the sound was getting louder by the second. Here and there a seaman held his hands to his ears as if to drown out that dread sound. Others tried to keep their nerve but their faces, coloured a blood red, revealed their fears all too clearly and all their chests heaved rapidly as if they were running a race. *Ping ... ping ... ping.*

"Motors above us, sir."

But they didn't need to be told by the operator, they could hear the rhythmic thud, thud of the hunter's engines all too clearly now as the destroyer sought them out, ready to kill in the blink of an eyelid. Someone gasped. A petty officer barked softly sensing the start of a panic, "None of that now, laddie!"

Witt wiped the sweat off his forehead with the back of his hairy paw. The whole world seemed filled with that roar, thud-thud. Wouldn't the damned Tommy go away?

"Engines receding, sir," the operator said, his voice husky with strain.

Witt sighed with relief. "They seem —"

His words were drowned by a tremendous roar. The U-boat reeled as if punched by a giant fist. Glass dials splintered. Cans of food rolled to the deck. In half a dozen places the plates buckled. Water started trickling in. In minutes the frightened ashen-faced crewmen were standing in water up to their ankles.

Again that great hammerblow on the hull. The lighting flickered on, off and then went out altogether. Someone yelled in fear. Witt took a grip on himself and ordered, "Emergency lighting! Hurry, emergency lighting!"

A petty officer cursed and stumbled. Next moment the lights came back on to reveal the chaos of the interior, water and wreckage everywhere, with a young blond sailor being sick with fear, his shoulders heaving violently as he retched miserably.

"Propellers approaching," the hydrophone operator sang out.

"Holy strawsack," someone cried. "Not again!"

"Enough of that!" Witt said sharply and tensed as the sound of the destroyer grew louder and louder. Again the thud-thud of engines seemed to fill the whole world. The U-boat's hull shook and trembled like a live thing with the vibrations. Here and there more men had that trapped look, their eyes wild with fear. Witt had seen it often enough before and knew if he didn't contain it it could lead to mass hysteria. But he no longer had the willpower to do so. It was taking him all his time to master his own fear.

"Engines directly overhead now, sir," the operator sang out and Witt noted the fear in his voice.

They waited, listening to that dread noise. Suddenly there were a series of soft plops. Something metallic grated against the submarine's outer hull. *"Grosser Gott-die Mine!"* someone cried. Another seaman started babbling the Lord's Prayer, his eyes screwed tightly close like a frightened child trying to blot out something very unpleasant.

Boom! The U-boat rocked violently. Plates splintered everywhere. Water flooded in. The lights went out. "We're sinking!" someone shouted, high and hysterical like a woman.

"Knock that off you cowardly sow!" an enraged petty officer shouted back. "None o' that, d'yer hear!"

Boom! Yet another mine exploded close by sending the U-boat reeling back and forth. More dials splintered. Suddenly there was an acrid smell coming from the engine room. Eyes filled with tears. In an instant men were coughing, retching and crying everywhere.

Witt knew what had happened. The batteries had ruptured, the fear of all submariners. Now they were giving off noxious gases. Something had to be done and fast. He looked around. The crew seemed at the end of their tether. Their shining eyes were desperate. He could hear just how much their chests wheezed as they fought for breath. He stared to where a petty officer had his hand on the flood valve to let in compressed air for surfacing, holding it with taut anxious fingers as if it were his only hope of salvation.

He made up his mind. "Stand by to surface!" he cried. "Start engines!" The engines coughed into life. More and more gas was flooding in. The U-boat began to rise.

"Up periscope!" Witt ordered.

There was an audible gasp from the ashen-faced crew. Witt staggered over to the instrument, his eyes filled with tears, his throat and chest burning with the gas. He straddled his arms above the rest. The glass cleared. He turned up the amplifier. There she was, the

Tommy, perhaps half a sea mile away and broadside on to the U-boat. Witt thought they might have a chance still.

"Down periscope," he commanded hurriedly. He didn't want the Tommies to spot the white wake of the instrument.

"Stand by three and four!"

"Three and four ready, sir," the torpedo mates yelled back.

"Up periscope."

The glass broke the surface again. The Tommy was turning rapidly now. She was coming in for another attack. He could see the sudden white fury at her stern as her props churned the water violently.

"Fire three!" he yelled his head swimming with the noxious gas. Then an instant later, "Fire four!"

The U-boat lurched violently as the two-ton torpedo zipped into the water followed one moment afterwards by the second "tin fish". Witt kept his eyes glued to the glass as his head whirled and whirled, and he felt he must blackout at any moment. Behind him in the boat the only movement was that of the grey opaque pearls of sweat trickling down the men's ashen faces and the harsh rapid gasps of their breathing.

Witt cursed. The destroyer was turning. She was racing away, a sudden white bone in her teeth. Would she escape?

"What's the matter, sir?" his Number One cried.

"The Tommy's trying —"

The rest of Witt's words were drowned by a thunderous explosion beneath the U-boat. A blinding blue flame seared the interior. Controls shattered. Glass splinters hissed through the air. The lighting flickered, went out and came on again as a gyro compass slammed against the bulkhead like a shell. Men screamed either with pain or fear. The U-boat tilted violently.

"Surface ... surface!" Witt screamed in panic. "Bring her up, now!"

The ratings jumped to their wheels. Spinning them round frantically they drove the water out of the tanks. They were sinking, they knew that. They had only seconds left. Air thundered into the tanks and they started to rise, the boat tilted at an alarming angle.

"Be ready to man the gun" Witt yelled, having enough reason left to remember the drill. "Stand by diesels."

"Let me take over, sir," his Number One pleaded.

Witt turned on him, face contorted with terror, eyes blazing and bulging out of his coarse face like those of a man demented. "Leave me alone, you shiteheel!" he shrieked.

The U-boat broke the surface, stern first. Witt clattered up the ladder and wrenched at the hatch. He emerged followed by a panic-stricken bunch of screaming yelling sailors. He flung it open. A burst of machinegun fire raked the conning tower. Witt reeled back holding his face. It was as if someone had just poked a red-hot poker in his eyes. He looked down at his hands to see if there was blood on them but he couldn't see them. For what seemed an age he just swayed there as the machineguns continued to rake the U-boat's casing and the frantic sailors pushed by him to the sloping deck waving towels and white undershirts in surrender crying, *"Nicht schiessen, bitte, nicht schiessen!"*

Suddenly Witt gave a banshee-like piercing howl. "I'm blind, I'm blind mates!" But no one was listening to Leutnant Ernst Witt any more.

Savage smiled as a great cheer went up from the crew, and the battered U-boat surfaced and the German ratings began to wave their tokens of surrender. He guessed that it was the U-boat's own torpedo which had broken her back. Perhaps it hadn't functioned when fired but as it sank the water pressure had actuated her motor. It seemed, he thought, poetic justice of a sort. Now one of those grey wolves which he so hated was there at last, surrendering with obscene bubbles of trapped air bursting all around her, gouts of thick diesel oil spreading outwards from her shattered, buckled plates.

"Stand by to pick up survivors," he commanded. "But keep your eyes peeled. The others might well be lurking around."

"Ay, ay, sir," his Number One snapped smartly and, clattering down from the bridge, he began to yell orders while the gunners in A and B turrets kept their 4.5 inch guns trained on the sinking U-boat and the panic-stricken survivors.

"Stop ports," Savage commanded, "wheel amidships. Steady as you go, half ahead together," Savage rapped out the commands as the deckhands under Number One's command leaned over the side trailing the scramble nets down towards the Germans, many of whom were wringing their hands and weeping with abject fear.

Minutes later they were pulling the last of the German survivors over the railing while fifty yards away the U-boat was slowly going under, air belching out of her conning tower, her metal plates buckling and rending as she went into her death throes.

Savage was in pain again yet his elation at this "kill" outweighed the pain in his chest. He knew that usually U-boat men were a tough bunch. After all, they were all volunteers and the cream of the German Navy. But he knew, too, from experience that if they were questioned immediately after capture when they had still not recovered from the violent shock of having their U-boat sunk under them they would talk, and he intended to make them talk.

"All right, Number One, bring in the captain."

"He's been badly hit, sir," his Number One interjected. "Blinded in both eyes the sick bay tiffy says."

"Can't help that, Number One," Savage said briskly, "and bring in his number one, too. Let's get at 'em as soon as possible."

"Ay, ay, sir," his Number One said rather wearily and wondered again just how brutal the captain could be.

Stationary directly below the destroyer, engines stopped, Brandt wondered now if he had done the right thing. He had seen the attack on Witt's boat and how the Tommy destroyer had almost stopped to pick up the U-boat's survivors. In those few minutes the Tommy destroyer had been the easiest target in the world. But if he had sunk her the survivors would have gone down with her, and he had been unable to allow that. "Damned idiot conscience," he said to himself, listening as above them the destroyer's engines started to thunder once more and she began to draw away. Now the overwhelming question was would the survivors talk and give the mission away?

It was a question to which Kapitanleutnant Brandt knew no answer. Fifteen minutes later he was underway once more, ploughing the sea heading west again, continuing the mission, though now his heart was full of dread uncertainties.

TWENTY-FIVE

"Break wireless silence, Number One," Savage said, his face very pale, lips a startling blue. The cross-examination had been tough and it had taken it out of him. The young second-in-command, a typical Hitler Youth fanatic, hadn't broken until Savage threatened to toss him over the side again. Then he'd talked.

"Ay, ay, sir," Number One responded, glad the cross examination was over, for he had not been quite certain that the skipper had been merely blustering when he had threatened to throw the arrogant young German to the sharks.

"Pick a low grade merchant marine code and report that, oh, you make up a ship's name, preferably foreign, Norwegian, something like that, report that you've sighted a German sub off Cape Cod. Beam it at Hyannis, that is the US Air Base closest to Cape Cod. That'll deal with the decoy."

"Ay, ay, sir. But why don't we alert the authorities in New York State about the other two German subs?" Number One asked, puzzled why he should be ordered to use a low grade merchant navy code and pretend to be sending the message from a merchantman.

"Because this is not just a battle action, Number One," Savage snapped, popping another nitroglycerine tablet under his tongue. "It's a political one, too. Remember Winnie wants to show the Yanks that the old Lion has still got teeth. If we allow the Americans to know fully what's been going on where is the kudos for the British Empire, eh? Let them have the honour of sinking the Cape Cod U-Boat while we destroy the other two and save New York or part of it at least. That'll give the Royal Navy and Mr Churchill a real standing with the ordinary American citizen, and by

God," he added grimly, "we need it the way the Yanks are trying to take over the world."

"I see now, sir," Number One said cheerfully. "I'll get Sparks to send it immediately, as soon as I've encoded the message. What about, "U-boat sighted X latitude. Am making my escape. Norwegian motor vessel ..." and then garble the name?"

Savage nodded, his mind already on other things. "Sounds all right to me. Right ho, Number One, jump to it."

Number One sped away.

As the pain in his chest started to ease Savage rose and stared thoughtfully at the chart of the American eastern seaboard on his desk. The picture was pretty clear now, although the young second-in-command had not known all the details. They had been reserved for the four U-boat commanders and Leutnant Witt, crazed with pain and shock at the loss of his eyes, had been reduced to talking gibberish. Still, Savage now knew about the decoy and that the other three boats of the Brandt Wolf Pack were to engage targets in New York with V-2 rockets.

He peered at the map of Greater New York and remembering a pre-war cruise when they had escorted the King Emperor and his Queen to that city in 1939, worked out the kind of targets the U-boats would be aiming for. They'd target prestige buildings with some kind of great symbolic significance to the average American, the Statue of Liberty and the like.

Now the question was, where would Brandt place his boats for the attack? He wished he could really break radio silence and ask the Admiralty for the details of the V-2's range, but he dare not. That would be giving away the game to the Americans who would be listening and would be reading their ally's code, as he knew they did routinely. Allies they might be, but both Britain and American both listened to each other's secret messages as a matter of course.

He had naturally read of the V-2s and knew they were now being fired from launching pads somewhere in Northern Holland, in the general area of Amsterdam it was thought. That would give them a range — he did some quick maths — of perhaps a couple of hundred miles if their target were London, which so far it had been.

He tugged at the end of his nose thoughtfully. Outside one of the cooks was singing tonelessly as he peeled spuds for the prisoners' meal, *"I've got balls that jingle-jingle-jangle,"* to the tune of a popular cowboy song of that winter, *"as we go riding merrily along."*

But would Brandt the ace risk missing a target by firing at that extreme range? Savage told himself he wouldn't. He was too much of a perfectionist. No, he'd take his Pack much closer than that so he'd get the hits he had come so far to achieve.

Outside the spud-bashing cook had changed to, *"Up came a spider/sat down beside her/whipped his old bazooka out and this is what 'e said, 'Get hold o' this, bash, bash/Get hold o' that/When there isn't a girl abaht and yer feeling lonely'."*

Savage shook his head and wished the damned cook would shut up; he couldn't hear himself think for the racket. Still he forced himself to concentrate, put himself in Brandt's shoes. No, Brandt definitely would come closer in than that. After all, Savage knew that Brandt had been with Leutnant Prien when in 1939 he had ventured into Scapa Flow itself, anchorage to the Royal Navy's Home Fleet, and had daringly sunk the battleship *Royal Oak* in full sight of the shore.

But where? Where would he surface to attack the greatest city in the United States, protected by a ring of naval and air bases stretching to south and north? It would have to be somewhere, where he had a chance of striking something of importance with his missiles and from whence he could make a quick getaway. For he knew from past clashes with Brandt that the German U-boat ace was not one of those fatalists in the submarine service who liked dicing with death and wasn't worried about getting the chop. Brandt, he knew for certain, wanted to come out of this alive if possible. So where?

There was a knock on the door. Savage frowned. "Come in," he barked.

It was his Number One. He saluted and announced, "Message sent. Sparks did his usual fiddle with his set so I don't think they'll be able to monitor where exactly the message came from. The Yanks asked for a repeat especially of the name of our vessel," he chuckled, "but Sparks went off the air tootsweet so the Yanks were out of luck."

"Do you think they bought it, Number One?"

"Very definitely, sir. The repeat signal was signed by a captain, none of that 'lootenant junior grade stuff'," Number One affected a fake US accent and smiled. "Oh yes, they bought it all right. "Spect they'll have already scrambled their planes at Hyannis."

"Good show, Number One. Thank you. Now then, here's our next problem. We've got to out-fox this Brandt fellow. There are still two U-boats of his at large and their target is New York. Now, if you were attacking the place, where would you position yourself?"

The two of them stared hard at the chart. Outside the spud-bashing cook was still singing as he peeled the mountain of potatoes. *"Tight as a drum never been done/queen of all the fairies,"* he was warbling away, *"Innit a pity she's only one titty to feed the baby/poor little bugger's got only one sucker ..."*

"If that cook doesn't stop singing in a minute," the captain threatened, "I'll have him on the rattle before he knows what's hit him."

"Well, you know what cooks are, sir," Number One said apologetically, as if that explained everything. "Back to our problem, sir. If I were the Jerry and wanted to knock off something important in New York I'd get in as close as possible."

"Why?"

"Simple, sir. The closer you get to the city itself and its harbour it's hardly likely that the Brylcreem boys," he meant the air force, "are going to loose their bombs on a sub. They are too close to the heart of the city. Look over there, that's Brooklyn and Manhattan over there. Further on Queens. I mean the place is packed with skyscrapers. What pilot's going to take a chance of dropping a bomb on the Statue of Liberty or the Empire State Building?"

"I see, I see. You're right, of course, Number One. Mind you, any U-boat skipper who went in that far would never get back to the open sea again. They'd be waiting for him out there in the Atlantic with a vengeance."

"Agreed, sir," Number One said, "but what if this fellow Brandt is a real fanatic like that young arrogant swine you just questioned? What if he does not give a damn about his own life? After all, any U-boat skipper who scuppers some of the world's tallest buildings will go down in history. The Huns would revere him for a thousand years to come just like they revere Attila the Hun for having sacked Rome."

Savage told himself that his Number One had got his history a little cock-eyed, but he had made his point effectively enough. "Of course, you're right. Brandt has always been a careful bloke, that's why he survived so long. But perhaps he's seen the writing on the wall for Germany and is prepared to go out in one last burst of glory."

"But that does put us in a bit of a fix, doesn't it, sir, a sort of a moral dilemma."

"How do you mean, Number One?" Savage demanded.

"Well, sir, if he does slip through and do his worst on New York because we failed to catch him, what are the Americans going to say about us?"

"I don't understand you."

"Put it like this then, sir. We should now alert the US authorities to Brandt's presence in the waters off the eastern seaboard, then they could throw in the full power of their navy, air force etc. to stop him before he ever gets anywhere near New York. If we don't —" the Number One shrugged and didn't complete the sentence.

Savage frowned. Of course, Number One was right. He didn't need a barrack room lawyer to explain what would happen if he failed to stop Brandt. There'd be all hell to pay. Britain would cop it right and proper from the Yanks. It would be as if the Yanks had sacrificed London when it could have been saved by British forces.

"But what am I going to do, Number One?" he said, a little note of pleading in his voice. "The PM has given express orders that the Yanks are not to be told in advance. It's not up to me to make decisions which are essentially top level and political."

"You could signal the Admiralty, sir?" Number One suggested. "Give them the position and let them make the decision."

"Well, that would certainly give away our position to the Hun. Their listening service would be on to us like a shot and they'd pass the info on to Brandt. He'd make good use of it to dodge us on that final run in. Besides, imagine how long it would take for their Lordships to reach a decision. They'd approach the PM for sure and then it'd be all jaw, jaw." He nodded to the calendar on the wall.

"Look at that, Friday 13 December. By dawn tomorrow, Saturday, we'll be off the US coast and —"

There was a sudden knock on the cabin door. Savage looked up annoyed, "Come," he barked.

It was Sparks, his hair tousled as if he had pulled off his earphones in a hurry and rushed up to the skipper's cabin without waiting to put on his cap as regulations prescribed.

"What is it, Sparks?"

"Just picked up a signal," Sparks said in his thick Yorkshire accent. "Can't read it like, sir cos it's in code. But I recognise the operator's handwriting all reet," he meant the manner of signalling. "It's that Jerry U-1226."

"You're sure?"

"Dead sure, sir."

"It's the decoy the young tough told us about, sir," Number One said excitedly. "Do you think he's broken radio silence because he's under attack?"

Before Savage had time to answer Sparks broke in with, "I think so, sir, cos the Jerry operator never ended the message."

"How can you know that Sparks, if the message was coded?" Savage demanded.

"Like, sir, their operators allus sign off with their signature. And the signature is allus in clear, saves time encoding, sir. The Jerry's on the U-1226 is 'JT' . I call him to mesen 'John Thomas', like he added cheekily using the naval euphemism for penis. Well this time he didn't give his 'John Thomas', that's why I think they was under attack."

"Thank you, Sparks. Good show. Next time wear your cap. Off you go."

Sparks, still grinning despite the rebuke, clicked to attention, did an extra smart about-turn and left, leaving the Number One staring at Savage. Finally, when the latter did not speak he could contain himself no longer. "Well, sir," he asked, "what will you do?"

Savage puffed out his lips and tugged the end of his big nose. "I've made my decision, Number One. I'm not going to signal their Lordships. We're going to find Brandt on our own. It's a chance, I know, but we'll have to take it."

Number One looked at Savage in dismay. "But if we fail, sir—"

"We will not fail, Number One," Savage cut him short harshly. "We'll get the bastard, never fear. Now these are my orders…"

TWENTY-SIX

"The rudder's gone, sir," the helmsman yelled above the noise of the exploding depth charges. "I've lost control."

"Try again!" Blau cried desperately, face crimson with fury and fear. "You've got to control her!"

Five minutes before they had been on the surface recharging the electric batteries for the last run-up to Cape Cod when the fighter-bombers had come roaring in at mast-top level. They had carried out an emergency dive but it had been no use. The American planes had spotted them all right. Bombs had come raining down. The U-1226 had been buffeted from side to side at the mercy of the enemy planes.

"Take her down, one hundred!" he had yelled above the racket.

Hurriedly the operators had pumped out the water and the U-1226 had sunk rapidly at an awkward angle with others fighting to get the trim right, and for a little while Blau had thought he had escaped his pursuers. But he had been wrong.

Minutes later depth charges dropped from flying boats had begun exploding all around the U-boat. "Take her down one fifty," he had ordered.

The U-boat had sunk another fifty metres while the off-duty watch stared with round apprehensive eyes, feeling their ears pop under the changed air pressure, waiting for the first plates to buckle. At one thirty they had begun doing so. Water started to trickle in. A couple of dials shattered sending flying glass everywhere. Abruptly the fetid air inside the submarine was filled with the stink of escaping chlorine. The batteries were beginning to leak. But at least they had left the depth charges behind.

Now, as the helmsman reported the rudder had gone, another series of depth charges timed to go off at a much deeper level were beginning to explode dangerously close.

Blau tried to calm himself. He had been in action before and had once endured a twelve-hour ordeal beneath the surface of the Black Sea. Then his nerve had almost cracked. Now he knew he couldn't stand a bombardment like that again. He'd break down.

He looked at the crew. They were all ashen-faced and sweating. All were breathing in short, hectic gasps as if their oxygen supply was already beginning to run short. But he knew it wasn't that. They were hyperventilating because they were scared, terrified even.

What was he going to do?

He daren't surface. The Ami pilots wouldn't give him a chance. They wouldn't allow him to surrender. They'd bomb him right out of the water.

Again a depth charge exploded above them. The U-1226 reeled and heeled violently. Broken crockery, tin plates, sodden paper slopped back and forth along the bottom of the boat. A man screamed as a rivet shot from one of the bulkheads and slammed into his face. Suddenly it looked as if someone had thrown a handful of strawberry jam at it. Panic was very near to the surface now.

Blau swallowed hard. The popping in his ears ceased for a few minutes. He had to think fast and hard. The main thing was to get away from his present position, he knew that. But with control of the rudder lost God only knew in which direction he would be steering. For all they would know they could be going around in circles. But there was no other way out. "Start both!" he cried above the hollow boom of another exploding depth charge. *"Quick now!"*

The petty officer pressed the starter button. The electric motors caught at once. There was a sudden steady hum.

"Both ahead!" Blau ordered, knowing there was not a moment to be lost.

His second-in-command looked at him aghast, "But we've no rudder, sir," he cried.

Blau ignored him, "Both ahead, *full!*" he commanded.

The revolutions picked up immediately. The U-1226 surged ahead. The sound of the exploding depth charges fell behind them. Blau felt a faint sense of hope. Perhaps they'd get out of this awful mess with a whole skin, he told himself. Suddenly he remembered the St Anton gymnasium back home in Mainz, the kids lining up dutifully for their music lessons, the Rektor, Dr Dirksen, beaming at them paternally through his pince-nez and patting his ample stomach, which he always did when he was pleased. God, what a fool he had been ever to volunteer for the submarine service for the sake of a dashing uniform and the silver dirk of a lieutenant! What wouldn't he give to be back there now! For the first time for six years he said a prayer: a prayer to the God he had once rejected back in 1938, to bring him back home safely to Mainz and the St Anton gymnasium.

He remembered where he was and that they were still not out of danger. "Take her up," he commanded. "One hundred."

The crew hurried to carry out his order. Slowly, unsteadily, the boat tilted at an angle. The U-1226 started to rise. Blau licked his parched, cracked lips. At least the mechanism worked. He held her at a hundred for a few minutes half expecting another shower of depth charges. None came.

"Take her up to periscope depth," he commanded, astonished at his own boldness. He was going to break surface. If they were there waiting for him he would be finished.

Slowly the U-boat started to rise. Blau waited tensely. "Periscope depth!" the petty officer sang out.

He steeled himself to give the command. "Up periscope," he barked in a voice which he didn't recognise as his own.

A hiss of compressed air and the periscope shot upwards. For the very last time, though he didn't know it at that moment, he twisted the gold-braided cap of which he had been so proud back to front and peered through the shining, calibrated circle of glass.

To his front, caught in the sickly white light of the false dawn, he saw the shoreline: a belt of brown sand with beyond a series of white clapboard bungalows from which no lights shone. He guessed they were summer holiday homes for the rich. Beyond there was a road with two cars moving along it very slowly as if there might be ice on the tarmac and the drivers were treading carefully. A seaside resort in winter, he concluded virtually dead, with the locals huddled around their stoves listening to boring radio programmes, waiting for the spring and life to start once again.

He turned on the intensifier and started to turn the periscope round. He saw it with startling suddenness hurtling out of the darkness, a slick silver shape coming at him at a tremendous speed. "Dive ... dive!" he shrieked in a frenzy of fear. *"Dive."*

The bridge exploded in a blinding flash. His body catapulted forward to smash against the periscope standards. His back was broken at once. For a long moment the spattered corpse hung between them, arms outstretched in helpless crucifixion before slowly slipping to the bloody deck. Leutnant zur See Blau, who with a bit of luck and no war might have lived out his life teaching the flute at a shabby suburban Rhenish gymnasium died as the U-1226 sank to the bottom off Cape Cod, the finger of the dead radio operator pressed to the key of his morse set, a spar skewered through his heart.

"We haven't a cat's chance in hell," Baeder cursed. "They're on to us. It's only a matter of time before they sink us as well."

Gloomily Number One nodded his approval as he dismissed the radio operator back to his set. He stared around the interior of the submarine and although the captain had not yet announced it, he knew the crew had already realised that something serious had gone wrong. He could see that from the despondent looks on their pale unshaven faces. "What should we do, skipper?" he asked.

Baeder, the ex-merchant marine skipper, ran his hand through his grizzled beard with a harsh rasping sound. "I'm a practical man, Number One," he said thoughtfully. "A man, I think, who knows when he's had enough. Besides, I've got these damned greenbeaks," he indicated the crew with a wave of his big paw, "to consider. They're all some mother's sons. Look at it like this: even if we did manage to carry out the mission successfully the Amis would hang the lot of us after the war, they'd string us up without compunction."

The Number One nodded his agreement. "You think we've had it, Germany I mean?" The junior officer knew he was expressing a thought that no one would have ever dared to speak in the Homeland with the Gestapo everywhere.

"Of course, Number One. The enemy's on both of Germany's borders. Do you think that Hitler can stop the Anglo-Americans and the Ivans at this stage of the game?" Baeder's face contorted scornfully. "Naturally he can't. The clock's in the pisspot and that's that. The Homeland's done for. So why make unnecessary sacrifices?"

"What's to be done then, skipper?" the Number One repeated.

"We could attempt to make a run for it," Baeder said thoughtfully, as if thinking aloud. "But I don't think we'd make it. The Amis and Tommies have got two of the Wolf Pack already." He stroked his beard once again. "No, there's only one way we're going to get out of this shitty mess, Number One."

The other officer looked at him hard and then said cautiously, "You mean, surrender, sir?"

"Yes, I do. It goes against the grain, but it's the only way out."

"I suppose so, sir," Number One said slowly as if the full implication was beginning to dawn upon him. He turned to face the expectant crew, faces hollowed out to death's heads in the eerie red light. "Kameraden, the captain has a statement to make."

Captain Baeder rubbed his grizzled chin once more and began without preliminaries. "We're surrendering," he said. "I have made my decision, so that is the way it is. I know, boys, it isn't going to be any fun being behind barbed wire for God knows how long. But it's better, believe me, than a watery grave. All right, that's it." He turned to the yeoman of signals. "Obermaat, I want you to send this."

"Sir."

"In clear. U-boat 1223 at latitude — the chief officer will give you the bearing in a minute — is now surfacing to surrender. Repeat, surfacing to surrender. Will fly white flag. Please do not instigate offensive action. Again repeat. Got it?"

"Got it."

As the signaller moved to his apparatus the U-boat skipper wiped his hands as if cleaning them of something. It was virtually all over. There was nothing more to be done.

Brandt looked thoughtful while next to him Number One waited, his mind racing, wondering what they were going to do now. They had picked up Baeder's signal in clear. Now it could only be a matter of minutes before the enemy replied and accepted the surrender of Baeder's boat. It seemed the mission was over. But what would the skipper do?

Brandt tugged at the end of his nose and finally broke the tense brooding silence. But when he spoke the words weren't the ones that the Number One expected. There were no recriminations, accusations, angry curses. Instead Brandt asked in a matter-of-fact manner, "Have you managed to work out Baeder's position, Number One?"

Surprised as he was by the question the other officer stuttered, "Yes ... yes, I have, sir."

"Excellent." Again Brandt lapsed into silence. There was no sound in the stationary submarine save for the rhythmic rattle of the pans in the little galley as the boat rocked gently from side to side in the water.

Suddenly Brandt started to speak in a low voice, almost as if he were talking to himself. "So Baeder's going to surrender, is he?" he said. "What will the Amis do? They'll send out a destroyer or something and perhaps a couple of aircraft as an escort. Where will they take him?" He sniffed. "To the nearest harbour and where is that?" He smiled thinly. "Our objective, New York."

"I don't quite understand, sir"

"Don't you see, Number One?" Brandt asked with sudden urgency. Leutnant Baeder is going to make a big entrance. All attention will be focused on the U-boat on the surface. No one will ever think that below his boat there will be another craft lurking which has no intention of surrendering. Indeed, its intentions are strictly dishonourable."

Number One stared at Brandt wide-eyed. "Do you mean —"

"I do ... I do," Brandt snapped. "Now, we'll waste no more time. Start motors, both ahead. Let's close up with Baeder. Come on now, *dalli dalli*. The good citizens of New York City are going to be in for a great surprise."

TWENTY-SEVEN

Hitler sat in the corner of the operations room rubbing his hands with glee. Elegant staff officers came and went bearing the latest messages from the new front. Telephones jingled. Teleprinters clacked. A general was shouting down the phone, "But the Remer Brigade must be in action at the latest eighteen hundred hours this Saturday! Do you understand?"

All was controlled chaos as the news of one American defeat after another in Belgium and Luxembourg came through. "The US 99th Division has broken and is in full retreat, general area of Rocherath ... Two regiments of the US 106th Infantry Division virtually surrounded, area of Bleialf-Schoenberg ... 110th Regiment, 28th US Infantry Division broken and running, along a line of Weiswampach and Vianden ... Fourth US Infantry Division evacuating positions along the River Sauer in Luxembourg ... " Everywhere it seemed the Americans were in full retreat. They had been caught completely by surprise. Now their thin line had been broken along a ninety kilometre front and the way to the River Meuse and the great port of Antwerp was wide open.

Linge, Hitler's valet, brought the Fuhrer a cup of peppermint tea and yet more tablets. The Fuhrer swallowed them without appearing to know that he was doing so. "A great day, Linge!" he cried, eyes sparkling with the drugs his doctors pumped into him. "This Saturday will go down in German history as the turning point of the war in the west, mark my words!"

"Jawohl, mein Fuhrer," his valet, who wore the uniform of a colonel in the SS, replied dutifully.

Hitler did not seem to notice his tall valet's coolness. "They're running, Linge," he announced excitedly. "The Amis are running everywhere! Those Jewish gangsters have no stomach for a real fight. This time we'll kick them out of Europe for good! What right have the Americans to determine the affairs of our Continent?"

"*Jawohl, mein* Fuhrer," Linge said again.

Schellenberg, cunning-eyed and clever, the chief of SS Intelligence, came across the room. "With your permission, *mein* Fuhrer, I should like to detail to you the latest reports from Obersturmbannfuhrer Skorzeny."

Hitler's eyes glistened even more and Linge wondered again how long the Fuhrer could survive on a diet of sixty pills a day and little food, for the Fuhrer's vegetarian diet made him break wind constantly so in consequence he ate little, living off his pills and peppermint tea. "Yes, I should like that very much, Obergruppenfuhrer Schellenberg."

Schellenberg flashed a glance at the sheaf of teletexts in his hand and then said, "Skorzeny's men disguised as American soldiers have penetrated the enemy's positions in depth. Several jeep loads of American-speaking teams are already on the River Meuse trying to find a suitable bridge for the SS armour."

Hitler clapped his hands together in sheer delight while at his feet the Alsatian bitch Blondi growled, eyes shut, at being disturbed. "Excellent ... excellent! Tell me more, Schellenberg."

"Our men in British captivity have broken out of their prisoner-of-war camps everywhere, in Scotland, in Northern England and in the region of London. Their clandestine radios report that so far they have not been able to seize arms but they are in process of doing so. Once armed they will march," he paused for dramatic effect, "on London!"

Hitler's face registered his absolute joy. "My God," he exclaimed, "that should put the fear of God into that sot Churchill! His whole damned house of cards is falling down about his ears. He tricked that Jew Roosevelt into getting into the war in order not to go under when I would have offered peace with dignity. Now he's about to lose his Empire and soon he'll lose the Americans, too. Well, Schellenberg, what of the attack on New York?" He looked up at the SS spy chief expectantly.

Schellenberg frowned. "I am afraid, mein Fuhrer, that I cannot report any success on that sector so far."

"No news at all?"

"Yes, *mein* Fuhrer. Some," Schellenberg hesitated. "Two of our boats have been sunk it appears and one —"

"Yes, go on, spit it out, Schellenberg," Hitler said urgently. "I am a man used to bad news, you know."

Schellenberg cleared his throat uneasily. "And a third has put out a signal in clear to say that it wishes to surrender, *mein* Fuhrer," he said hastily, avoiding looking at Hitler.

"Surrender! My U-boat captains do not surrender!" Hitler exploded.

Discreetly Schellenberg moved back a pace as if he half expected Hitler to throw the cup of peppermint tea at him. But Hitler didn't. Instead he asked, "Is not Kapitanleutnant Brandt still at large?"

"Yessir," Schellenberg said hastily, glad that the expected explosion had not materialised. "Grossadmiral Doenitz assures me that Brandt is still at liberty with his boat. There have been no reports from him or about him from Allied sources."

Hitler's frown vanished. "I know Brandt of old. Why, he was with Prien in 1939 when they sunk the *Royal Oak* in Scapa Flow right at the heart of the Royal Navy's greatest base. If anyone can do it, it will be Kapitanleutnant Brandt."

The signaller turned off the loudspeaker and the excited voice of the speaker at Radio Berlin shouting out the new victories in Europe — so many thousand Americans captured, whole divisions overrun, panzers driving deep into Belgium — died away. The crew looked strangely sombre, not impressed by what seemed great successes five thousand kilometres away. They had nothing to do with their world encased in this stinking metal coffin just off the coast of the United States. By now they all knew of Baeder's intention to surrender. Brandt had always been strictly honest with his crews. It was the best way to command, he thought, tell the men the situation without pulling punches and then tell them what he was going to do. That was genuine leadership he had always maintained.

Now Brandt knew the time had come to tell the men what he did intend to do. "Comrades," he said without preamble, not even raising his voice. "You've heard what is happening on the other side of the pond. At this moment our comrades of the Army are fighting, and dying, for the Homeland. We can't let them down by not doing something after we have got this far."

He let the words sink in for a few moments noting that some of the petty officers, his "old hares" as he called them, men not noted for their enthusiasms, were nodding their heads as if in agreement.

"Now you know," he continued, "I am not one for wasting lives. But we have to do something. What?" He answered his own question. "We shall surface and fire one missile. Just one. It will take a matter of minutes. Then we bolt for it in the general confusion. Not back across the Atlantic, though." He shook his head firmly. "We wouldn't stand a cat's chance in hell of making it back to Lorient. No, we shall trick the Amis. Instead of Lorient we shall head for Mexico."

"Mexico?" one or two of the men exclaimed in surprise.

"Yes, Mexico," he repeated firmly. "Some two hundred sea miles, perhaps twenty-four to twenty-six hours sailing time and then we'd be in Mexican territorial waters. There we surrender, for Mexico is neutral and I am sure in due time our embassy people there will see that we are repatriated. Even if it can't be done in hurry I am sure that none of you will object to a few months in the sunshine scoffing as many oranges as you want and sporting with the local female population." He grinned.

They grinned, too. The potentially tense situation had been defused.

He allowed them a few moments to absorb the surprising news then his face hardened again and he was very business-like when he spoke once more. "Leutnant zur See Baeder has signalled in clear that he will surrender to the enemy at dawn. Obviously he is taking no chances. He wants to be clearly identified by the enemy. Now I calculate our present position is two sea miles from Baeder's. He is proceeding underwater at a fairly slow speed." He paused, before he gave it to them. "We shall now proceed to catch up with Baeder's boat and join him when he sails to surrender!"

***

"Well," Savage demanded his eyes burning. "What are the Yanks doing, Number One?"

"That surrender message must have caught them completely with their knickers down, sir," the other officer replied cheerfully. "Sparks says that the airways are buzzing with messages to and fro from naval headquarters and Washington. They've had Jerry subs off this coast before, lots of them back in '42, but never one which offered to sail up the Hudson and surrender. That is really one for the book."

Savage looked sour. "You don't have to be so damned chirpy about it, Number One," he exclaimed.

"Sorry, sir."

Savage looked out through the bridge shield. To the east the dark sky was beginning to break up. A dirty white light was starting to glow. Soon it would be dawn and the German submarine would surface. He frowned and his Number One said, "What are we going to do sir?"

"Well, Brandt must have heard that message in clear as well. Therefore the question is what is *he* going to do?"

"Well in a way, sir, our tame U-boat ace is between the devil and the deep blue sea. He can't go in now, sir, because the Yanks know he's there, and he can't go back because he'd never survive three thousand miles of the Atlantic with the whole of the US Navy looking for him."

"Exactly. But you know Number One, the reason that Brandt has survived so long is because he's always weighed up the pros and cons carefully. I'm sure he knows he's in a devil of a fix and is at this very moment trying desperately to wiggle out of it." Savage saw the unspoken question in his Number One's eyes. "So as a first thing we're going to close up with that sub intending to surrender."

"Ay, ay, sir. I'll give the order."

"And another thing," Savage added almost as an afterthought, "I want all the asdic operators at their posts. No stand down. I want them listening for that sub even if it is about to surrender. It's just a hunch, Number One, but I'm not taking any chances."

"Ay, ay, sir." Then his Number One was off to carry out his order telling himself that if they did get to berth in New York he'd spend a month's pay on nylons and perfume. There was a nice little Wren officer who looked very tidily in black, unregulation, nylons and had a particularly exciting way of showing her gratitude. Suddenly Number One was very happy; it was virtually all over, at last.

Savage wasn't. His chest hurt like hell again and he felt a sense of let-down, even failure. They'd definitely board him when they returned to the UK. It was no use kidding himself that he wasn't extremely sick. He knew it. But, by God, he would have liked to have had the satisfaction of sinking Brandt before he was beached. That would have rounded off the war for him, very nicely.

He thought once more of Mary, his wife, lying there naked in a bath of her own blood that terrible day in Southsea in what now seemed another age. He had not had another woman since. He had shut all that business firmly out of his mind since 1940. For four years he had concentrated totally, one hundred per cent, on killing Germans. It had been his revenge for the way they had ruined his life. Now the violence was over and in due course their Lordships would pension him off to a slippered, semi-invalid retirement in some boring coastal town like bloody Bognor Regis. It didn't seem fair.

"Sir, sir," Number One, his face flushed with excitement, burst into his sombre reverie.

Savage turned a little startled. "What is it, man?" he demanded.

"The asdics, sir," Number One gasped.

"What about them?"

Number One fought to get his breath. "They've picked up pings."

"Pings?"

"Yes, two of 'em, two separate pings."

"Christ Almighty," Savage yelled. "It's Brandt. He's down there with the one who's going to surrender. Number One," he roared, "Sound action stations. We're going to get the bugger after all!"

TWENTY-EIGHT

Dawn. Saturday December 16, 1944.
In the city the news vendors were getting their stands ready for the early workers and those coming off the night shift at the defence plants. Steam gushed from the manhole covers as with frozen fingers they wrote up the headlines. HODGES HITS SIEGFRIED LINE AGAIN; PATTON DRIVES INTO SAAR, they read, detailing places most New Yorkers had never heard of till now. LONDON TAKES MORE V-2S they read, too, but that was far away. Here in cosy if cold New York most thought was of the coming Christmas, the last of the war in Europe people were saying. Certain goods were scarce but there was plenty of money about, earned in the booming defence industry; they'd have a good time all right, no doubt about that. Slowly the dawn haze started to vanish. A cold ball of winter sun came out colouring the New York skyline, immense and imposing, a deep blood-red.

Baeder drew a deep breath. If the Gestapo ever laid their hands on him he knew he would be strung up for defeatism without trial. But there was no other way. "Periscope depth," he ordered. All around the solemn-faced crew tensed.
The boat rose. Now the U-boat men could hear the ping-ping of the enemy asdic bouncing off the submarine's casing quite clearly. "They've got us, Number One," Baeder said.
His Number One nodded solemnly but did not speak. His mind was too full.

"Up periscope," Baeder commanded. The pinging was getting ever louder.

Smoothly the periscope slid up its polished metal tube. Baeder shoved his cap round telling himself that this was probably the last time he would ever do so. His career as a U-boat skipper was over. He hung his arms over the supports and peered through the periscope. There it was, the New York skyline. He had seen it before but it never failed but to impress him. He adjusted the intensifier. The image grew even larger. There they all were: the Empire State Building; the Rockefeller Center, the Chrysler Building; all those symbols of the New World which they had thought they could beat. Now he knew *they* were beaten instead.

Ping-ping ... *ping-ping,* the sound was getting on his nerves. They were surrendering. What in three devils' name was wrong with the Amis? They didn't need to hunt his boat now! All he wanted to do was to get the mess over with swiftly and peacefully. "Stand by to surface," he commanded.

The klaxon shrieked. But its electrical wail could not quite drown the noise above. Even without the aid of the hydrophone the crew of the U-boat knew that the surface vessel was almost on top of them. Baeder swung the periscope round. He gasped with horror.

A destroyer, a white bone in its teeth, was heading straight at the spot where he would emerge, going at least thirty knots! "Heaven, arse and cloudburst!" Baeder exploded. "What is the fool up —" He didn't complete his sentence. Instead he cried in sudden alarm, "Dive ... dive ... dive!"

The sharp prow of the destroyer smashed directly into the exposed periscope. The U-boat reeled madly. Abruptly it was out of control and surfacing at a crazy angle.

Baeder made a wild snap decision. "Abandon ship!" he screamed as the water started to pour in at the conning tower. The lights flickered, went .out, came on again and then extinguished for good.

"Emergency lighting!" the Number One yelled above the panic "Stand fast, wait for the lights —" Something hit him a savage blow in the face and he went reeling back into the water flooding the base of the interior.

Now it was every man for himself. Somehow Baeder got the hatch to the conning tower opened as the water continued to pour in drenching the screaming, terrified men as they clawed and tugged at each other in their attempts to get up the ladder before it was too late.

Gasping, as if he were running a great race, Baeder flung himself over the side of the conning tower into the icy dawn air. Man after man followed. The destroyer had wrecked the whole superstructure of the U-boat. Metal and tangled wire lay everywhere and she was sinking rapidly.

He flung a look to stern. The destroyer, the white ensign of the British Navy streaming proudly at her stern, was turning in a tight wild-white T. She was coming in again, for the kill. There was nothing for it he told himself instantly. "Abandon ship!" he yelled as the destroyer, now turned, opened up with quick firers, white tracer hurtling towards the battered U-boat at a tremendous speed. *"Aller Mann verlassen das Schiff!"*

Next to him a petty officer screamed and flung up his arms as if he were climbing the rungs of an invisible ladder, a series of blood-red buttonholes stitched the length of his brawny chest. Next moment he hit the littered deck, dead.

A moment later Baeder was hit himself. The impact knocked him into the water, arms flailing, blood jetting in a scarlet arc from his shattered chest. He screamed and went under to come up spluttering and treading water.

Another shell pattern raked the length of his sub. It was sinking rapidly now, with heads bobbing up and down in the oily water everywhere, the men crying frantically for help in the icy cold. "Help us!" Baeder cried fervently in English. "Why do you not help us? We are no danger —"

The words died on his lips for the destroyer was flashing by them, cutting through the channel at speed, her screws churning the water to her stern into a frothy bubbling white. Here and there those in her path calmly accepted their fate, chewed to pulp by those flashing propellers. Others swam frantically to escape before it was too late.

Slowly, feeling the strength ebb out of his big body rapidly, Baeder turned his head to see where the swine of a Tommy who had so cruelly abandoned his crew was heading. Now he saw the reason for the destroyer's frantic haste.

Brandt's U-boat was slowly emerging from the water, the hatches already opened on the deck with the tip of the V-2 missile clearly visible.

Dying as he was, Baeder felt angry resentment well up inside his shattered body. "The bastard," he cursed, knowing now why the Tommy skipper was acting so brutally. Brandt had used his attempt at surrender to cover his own penetration of New York harbour. Somehow the Tommy had detected him and how he was heading for the kill. "Damn you, Brandt," he choked, mouth filled with hot blood. "I hope he sends you to hell ..." Then he went under for good.

Suddenly Brandt spotted the destroyer bearing down on him, racing past the sinking Baeder boat. "Both engines ahead!" he yelled urgently.

The U-boat leapt forward. At the deck gun the crew snapped into action. Behind Brandt on the conning tower the twin spandaus joined in. Now all was frantic haste as the submarine swung round, churning up an arc of wild water behind her, guns blasting away. Now virtually the whole of the great missile had emerged from below. It would be only a matter of minutes before its crew fired it and at that range they couldn't miss; they had the whole of New York's skyline to choose from.

Desperately Savage's gunner's opened fire. A shell glanced off the submarine's bow. She reeled wildly. A hole appeared in the casement. Fist-sized red-hot metal scythed through the air. A gunner screamed and went over the side. His severed head rolled into the scuppers like a child's abandoned football.

"Get that missile team," Savage yelled frantically as the V-2 started to swing round, levelled at the centre of the New York skyline. "Quick ... before it's too late!"

The gunners in B-turret, hooded like monks in anti-flash gear, swung their turret round, depressing the twin 4.5 inch guns at the same time. The submarine with its deadly missile reared up filling the gunlayer's sights. He tensed, feeling the sweat trickling down the small of his back. "Guns closed up," the petty officer sang out. The gunlayer tried to calm his tense breathing. He couldn't afford to miss. There wouldn't be a second chance; he could see the Jerry gunners at the missile preparing to fire, too. He had to hit the damn thing.

"*Fire!*" the petty officer yelled.

He pressed the button. The twin guns roared into action. Noise and smoke filled the turret. Instinctively the gunner blinked and prayed. Up on the bridge Savage flung up his glasses, the terrible pain in his chest forgotten. If the unknown gunner didn't succeed with his salvo war would be returning to the American east coast for the first time in almost a century.

There was a burst of dark smoke. In its centre there appeared a spurt of cherry red flame. The U-boat reeled crazily but still kept on coming — for an instant. Suddenly, startlingly, there was a tremendous explosion. The shock wave made the destroyer tremble. All around the muddy water was whipped up into a white frenzy.

The U-boat shuddered wildly now. Thick black smoke, licked with flame, poured from her shattered diesels. Unseen by the awed spectators in the water and those on the destroyer one of her engines ignited. Awe-struck, his pain forgotten, Savage felt the searing heat strike him in the face.

Scarlet flame jetted out in a gigantic, all-consuming blow-torch, ripping across the boat and over the water. Desperately the survivors of Baeder's boat tried to escape the funeral pyre. In vain: one by one they were overtaken by that great flame. They disappeared dying and searing beneath the boiling water.

Dying on his feet, his other arm blown off by the explosion, a helpless lost Brandt croaked hoarse commands. But around him in the shattered conning tower all were already dead. It was hopeless. Suddenly, as he sagged there, feeling the life blood ebb out of his broken body, he thought of Gerda. Slowly, infinitely slowly, his blackened face broke into a weary smile and for a fleeting moment he was happy. Then he was dead.

Another explosion racked the U-boat. It was all that was needed to finish her off. Almost casually she rolled over like a dead whale, exposing her ugly red-painted belly. With one last flurry of white water she slipped below the water and was gone, forever.

"Half speed," Savage commanded in a low voice.

The destroyer slowed down. In awed silence the deck crew stared at the floating wreckage drifting by in the dirty water. It was all there was to signify that only moments before there had been two German U-boats just off America's greatest city, ready to bring the five-year war to the United States at last.

Savage stared at a great hunk of salt pork in a muslin cover drifting past and shook his head as if in wonder. Next to him an equally awed Number One finally broke his silence to say, "Well, we've done it, sir, haven't we?" It was not a statement but a question: one of doubt and uncertainty.

Savage popped another tablet under his tongue, for the pain was back again with a vengeance. "I suppose we have," he said very slowly and without any note of triumph in his voice. Indeed his tone was of infinite weariness. "I suppose we have."

Over from the piers where the great liners had tied up before the war a launch was coming out towards them fast, sirens wailing angrily. It was followed by a grey naval blimp, its crew firing red flares. From port and starboard other grey naval craft were hastily leaving their anchorages and heading for the slow-moving destroyer.

Savage shook his head as if coming out of a trance. "All right, Number One, prepare to heave to."

"Ay, ay, sir," Number One said miserably the vision of the nubile naval Wren clad only in black nylons vanishing swiftly.

"Yes, Number One, now we're going to face the music ..."

ENVOI

In the event Captain Savage, DSO and DSC, didn't "face the music". The head of the US Navy, Admiral King, who fervently hated "the Limeys" as he always called the British, wanted Savage court-martialled immediately. His fellow chiefs-of-staff said it was technically impossible; Savage didn't belong to the American service. Besides, with the great battle now raging in Europe they didn't want any trouble with their British ally, especially as a British general, Field Marshall Montgomery, was commanding the bulk of the US troops engaged in that battle.

King appealed to President Roosevelt as commander-in-chief of the US Military. Roosevelt, who didn't like King, turned him down flatly. King threatened he might "go public". Coldly Roosevelt told him that if he did it would be he, King, who would be court-martialled. There the matter ended and an immediate "top secret" was placed on the whole affair.

So Captain Savage was allowed to return to Britain. Because of the American outrage over what had happened at Sandy Hook he was not awarded any decoration. But he was received by Churchill. The Prime Minister was in high good humour. He gave Savage a cigar, Savage didn't smoke, and a very large whisky, although it was ten in the morning. With an impish smile on his moon-like face, Churchill said, "Let our American cousins rant and rage, Captain. But you've certainly shown them that the old British Lion is not altogether toothless, yet. Thank you, Captain Savage, for what you have done."

With Churchill's blessing Savage went back to sea. So he was never forced into that slippered retirement in "bloody Bognor Regis". He died as he had always wished to die since that fateful day in 1940 at Southsea, fighting Germans. On 1 January 1945, his destroyer was ambushed just off Harwich by a flotilla of fast E-boats. For two hours the light German craft roared and raced around the much slower destroyer like a pack of angry grey wolves trying to pull down a larger prey. Time and time again the lone destroyer dodged their torpedoes by a hair's breadth. But in the end Savage's luck, and that of the whole ship's crew, ran out. The destroyer took a torpedo midships. She broke up at once and went down with all hands. There were no survivors save, strangely enough, the ship's cat found floating on a spar many hours later.

As for the two conspirators, Skorzeny and Schellenberg, they survived but later they went to their deaths taking their secret with them. Understandably. So today there is no one left alive who knew the secret of *Unternehmen Seeadler* or Sea Eagle, as it was originally called in Germany.

So if diver Edward Michaud does ever manage to get permission to raise the U-1226 and finds what it is really carrying, and I strongly doubt he ever will, he'll uncover a story that will put all Mr Grisham's thrillers very much in the shade. I mean who would ever dare write a story, even fictional, about the day that the Manhattan skyline was almost blown from the face of the earth?

THE END

If you enjoyed this book, look for others like it at Thunderchild Publishing: https://ourworlds.net/thunderchild_cms/

Made in United States
North Haven, CT
24 November 2023